MAKING
SCENE S

ALT-X Press
229 St. John's Place Suite 4c
Brooklyn, NY 11217

ISBN 0-9703517-0-4

Portions of this novel were published earlier in the following anthologies: *To Honor a Teacher* (Andrews McMeel), *Scream When You Burn: An Anthology of Southern California Writers* (Incommunicado Press). Portions of this novel were published in the following magazines: *Alt-X, ArtScope, Blood & Aphorisms, Caffeine, Driver's Side Airbag, Iowa Review Web, !Kung, Le-champignon, Naked Poetry, The Mezzanine Reader, Mississippi State's FineArt Forum, Prism International, Thirteenth Moon, Whiskey Island Review,* and *3AM Magazine.*

MAKING
SCENE S

adrienne eisen

Melanie —

Adrienne Eisen

I ANNOUNCE that I am no longer accepting money from my family.

I move to Chicago, to an apartment with a small room, a small kitchen, and a closet big enough to put my mattress on the floor.

I write a letter to my advisor thanking him for all the honors-student-research-money he finagled for me during the last four years, and p.s. I withdrew all my applications to graduate school—I want to play professional beach volleyball.

The only thing I can find in the want ads that won't interfere with volleyball is modeling. When I call, they tell me to send some seminude snapshots, "Because some girls are naturals and some need lots of training."

On Friday, I take the El to my parents' house. After dinner and prayers for Shabbat, my parents try to convince me to take their money. I tell them I am going to model nude to pay my rent. Mom says I'm wasting my education and volleyball is a sport, not a job. Dad says to go to the upstairs living room and he'll take the pictures, but he thinks what I'm doing is wrong.

In the living room, he fiddles with the light switches to create an expensive eating-place atmosphere. I put on my bikini, and he starts clicking.

"Let's do this fast," I tell him. "I want to get out of here."

At first I just lie there while he takes the pictures. But after a few minutes I feel comfortable, like I've been doing this my whole life. I start hamming it up. We try lots of stuff, standing, sitting, hanging. He tells me he's running out of film, which is good because I'm having trouble thinking of more stuff to do. For the last shot he ties my arms above my head with his belt and I struggle to get loose.

CAMERON AND I are leaning back on our hands in the sand, and when he shifts his weight, more sand covers my hand. I want to feel his fingers, but I don't move mine because he's dating Julie again. The whole time I was away at school bragging about dating a doctor five years older than I am, he was here in Chicago still in love with Julie.

"Cameron," I say, "there's a co-ed tournament this weekend. Can we play together?"

"You should play women's," he says. "You're so much more powerful on a women's net. The men's net is too high."

"I don't know how to find a woman to play with. I don't know anyone. Will you just play?"

"Yeah. Okay, but people just need to see how good you are. Be sure to cover half the court this game so they see you can hit."

When it's our turn, we warm up on the court. Cameron introduces me to the man and woman we're playing. Cameron says, "You can serve both of us."

The other man says, "We usually only serve the man."

Cameron says, "Well, we both play, so you can serve both of us."

I love Cameron.

He pats my butt when he gives me the ball to serve, and I get a chill.

When he dives, I wipe the sand off his back, slowly.

He tickles me when I hit into the net so I don't have a chance to get mopey.

We lose. We were winning, but they started serving me every ball, and then we lost.

"Sorry we lost," I say.

"Pasta?" he says.

"I can't believe you still have any pasta after making pasta for us three nights in a row."

"I bought more pasta."

Cameron screens his calls while he stirs his pasta, and Julie leaves a message: "Hi Cam. I thought I'd come over and give you a blow job, but I guess you're not home."

Cameron laughs.

I would be too shy to say that to him.

"Cam?" I say.

"Yeah?"

"I've never heard anyone call you Cam."

"She's the only one who does, I think."

I go to his bathroom and brush my teeth with the door open so he knows I am still brushing after meals and I still need to have my toothbrush there.

He drives me back to my apartment. I look at his profile. He has perfect posture and perfect eyebrows, and a ski-slope Protestant nose.

He stops in front of my building and leans over to kiss me.

"What are you doing?" I say. "We can't kiss. You're dating Julie."

"So? I'm not married to her."

"Well, I can't just casually kiss. I have to be important to someone."

"You are," he says. "You're my favorite volleyball partner."

"Thanks," I say, and I slam the car door. I do it dramatically, and when he drives away, I fall over because my beach bag is caught in the door.

I CAN'T SLEEP and I feel like I'm wasting my time in bed. I look over at the clock—only 6 a.m.

I go down to Seven-Eleven. I go slowly, thinking there must be some way to avoid starting off another day with such lack of control. When I get to the store, the clerk says, "Hi." Some days I come here three times.

I love bagels, but they're too hard to throw up, so I can't buy them now. I grab a box of vanilla creams and a box of chewy chocolate chips. Then I pick up a pint of whole milk. I like skim, but whole milk is like stomach grease. It makes everything come up more smoothly.

I glance down at what I've collected. I worry maybe there's not enough food. I get a tube of Pillsbury frozen sugar cookie dough which comes up easily every time.

Sometimes I steal the food, because it upsets me to think how much money I spend on food. But today I feel like paying.

I eat some cookies on the way back to my apartment to make the walk seem shorter. Everything is easier when I'm eating.

When I get back to my apartment, I sit down at my desk and eat. I eat all the cookies and finish half the tube of cookie dough and then my stomach starts to hurt. I take the rest of the food to the incinerator, and sit back in the chair to wait; right after my stomach stops hurting is the best time to vomit because the food is mushy enough to come up smoothly, but almost nothing has had time to leave my stomach.

I tell myself I'll never do this again.

I take off all my clothes and lean over the toilet. I stick my finger down my throat as far as it will go and wiggle it around. The cookie dough comes out. I throw up until I think I've gotten almost everything. I reach down into the toilet and squish the vomit to see what's come up. I'm always careful not to heave too many extra times because I read that extensive vomiting can ruin the esophagus. My worst nightmare is that I'll have to go to the hospital with a torn esophagus.

My body has a feeling of relief and my head feels light. I feel very accomplished. I brush my teeth twice and rinse off my body in a cold shower. I go back to bed and pull the covers up to my chin. I feel calm and peaceful.

MY MOM DROPS OFF an answering machine and a bag of food and some plants.

"No," I say. "No plants. I don't want to take care of anything."

"This apartment is too depressing," she says.

"Then don't come visit."

"Don't be fresh."

"I don't want plants, Mom. Please. I don't want any plants."

"Okay. I'll take care of them at our house until you decide you want them."

I am silent.

She says, "I want you to set up that answering machine as soon as I leave. I'll call you when I get home. There's kugel in the bottom of the bag. You should eat it tonight, before it goes bad."

"Hi. You've reached 359-8213. If you're calling to find out what I'm doing with my life, don't leave a message."

I redo the message to include the area code.

It's too dark to play volleyball, so I read. I read on the floor, leaning against the wall, amidst piles of books I bought during college when all I had time to read was Machiavelli and other theories of justice. I'm reading what I choose now, and I'm doing it six hours a day.

I keep telling myself I'll go out and get a job after I finish the book I'm reading. So I curl up in a corner and before I finish the last of *Ethan Frome*, I take out a slice of kugel and start *House of Mirth*. But there's something wrong with the kugel — it's been bad for a very long time.

CAMERON IS LYING on the towel next to me. It's my towel, because he forgot his towel. After the tournament my towel will smell like him. We're both on our stomachs and we're resting our heads on our arms, faces turned toward each other. I love tournaments because we have to wait for our games and there's nothing to do but lie on the sand next to each other.

Cameron is telling me about the ER two nights ago. One guy came in with a McDonald's cup stuck up his butt.

I am wondering if Cameron likes having our faces so close. I am thinking about the end of today, when I'll start waiting for the weekend again.

When he finishes his story, he says, "Do you think we should scout the next team we play?"

"No," I say, "I'd rather just lie here."

"What happened to all your feistiness? What happened to your must-win instincts?"

"They're here," I say, "somewhere."

I BRING MY PICTURES to the photographer, and he says he likes my body but I look a little stiff.

"I think I just need some practice," I say.

"Well, stand up. Let me see you pose."

I don't want to ask what to do, but I can't imagine what he wants. Or maybe I can imagine: "Well, like what?"

"For starters, you have nice legs, but if you stand on your toes, your legs look better." I stand on my toes. "See," he says, "you're just standing there. You're too inhibited."

I leave and I'm totally pissed. I can't believe I'm too fucking inhibited; I'll never be able to turn on a man for real if I can't even do it for money.

I go back to my apartment and practice naked, in front of the mirror, opening my mouth, and arching my back, and putting my hands in my hair. Then I fantasize that I'm posing for the *Playboy* centerfold, and there are forty men standing around, telling me what to do. I'm doing it better than they ever imagined; they all jerk off while they watch me. And I have the most literate-written interview in the history of the *Playboy* centerfold.

"WHAT ARE YOU DOING tonight?" Cameron asks.

"Nothing," I say.

"Do you want to go to Kingston Mines?"

"Okay."

"Do you know what it is?"

"No."

"It's a blues club. If you're going to live in Chicago, you've got to know where the blues clubs are."

Buddy Guy plays and the tables vibrate. Cameron catches me

looking at him three times. He yells over the music, "Do I have snot hanging from my nose?"

"I'm just looking around," I yell back.

On the way home, I tell Cameron I'm thinking I'm a lesbian, which I really am thinking, but I'm telling him because I don't want him to know I'm craving him when he's not craving me. "Tall blondes," I say. And Cameron turns his brown-haired head to me and smiles.

"Yeah?" he says.

"Yeah. Are you surprised? I mean, do you think I'm a lesbian?"

"Not the way you were in bed with me. But maybe you should just try it."

"Well, I'm thinking of that, but I'm scared. I don't know how to do it."

"There are a lot of gay nurses in the ER. I could hook you up. Tall, blond nurses."

"Cameron, why are you smiling?"

"I can't believe this is the person who told me she couldn't have sex during her period because the Torah forbids it."

"Yeah. But I wouldn't say that again," I say.

He pulls up to my building and says, "See you later."

IT TAKES ME TWENTY MINUTES to find this guy on my map: He's in between the State of Illinois Building and Marshall Fields. Inside his apartment is large and white.

He shows me some of his work, and I compare my body to each of the women he has pictured. He says he notices I take longer looking at the pictures with two women.

I wonder if this means I'm a lesbian.

He says, "I know a girl you'd go great with."

"These aren't real couples?"

"No, they just get together for the shoot. Usually I pick 'em good, though, and they want to keep going longer than the shoot. Sometimes they go home together. That's what I'm all about—I want you girls to have fun."

"Uh-huh." I keep looking at the pictures.

"Would you be interested in me setting you up?"

I don't trust him. But I don't know how else I'd ever get to have sex with a woman. I think about it while I finish looking through the third album. I wish there were more.

He has me sign a release.

"What's this for?" I ask.

"Sometimes I sell pictures to *Penthouse*."

"I'll be in *Penthouse*?"

"Don't worry. It's soft focus." He shows me pictures of fuzzy, unidentifiable women.

I sign.

He gives me a robe to change into. I come out of the bathroom with my shoes in one hand and my clothes and his robe tucked under my arm. "I don't need this," I say, and I hand back his robe. "What do you want me to do?"

He says, "Just lie down on the bed and enjoy yourself." I lie down, but I don't know how he wants me to enjoy myself, so I ask. He says, "Maybe you'd like some oils and lotions to put on your—"

"No," I say, "I'm fine."

He says, "Just do what you'd normally do alone in bed."

So I start masturbating. But when I masturbate, the only thing that moves is my index finger and my clitoris. He tells me to rub my stomach and my thighs, which means I have to stop masturbating, but he doesn't see it that way, and he clicks clicks clicks.

I go home and I leave a message on Cameron's machine that I paid this month's rent by posing for *Penthouse*. I say it casually, like I do this kind of stuff all the time.

ON MONDAY, it's drizzling, but I go to the beach anyway. I don't know what else to do. The walk there is wetter than I expected, and the beach is bare. On the way back I buy five Hostess apple pies, and when I get very close to my apartment I buy some Ding Dongs.

At home I throw up, and I scrape the back of my throat with my fingernail. I finish throwing up, and blood comes out. I think it's the scrape, but just in case, I put all my dirty clothes in the laundry basket before I get into bed.

THE MAN HAS TO PICK ME UP because he lives in some suburb that I've never heard of. He comes with his wife in a minivan, and she gets out to let me in. He's paralyzed from the waist down.

On the way to their house, I'm a college graduate. The wife asks me how many books I've read, and I say two thousand and thirteen. The husband asks me where I grew up, and then he says, "Can't your parents give you money?"

"I want to be independent," I say.

"Do they know you model?"

I say, "No."

Their house is small and they've turned the dining room into a makeup room and the living room into a shooting gallery.

They want to show me photo albums so I know what they like. I sit on the sofa, next to the woman, and the man narrates from his wheelchair. He likes clothes that fit narrowly and legs that spread widely. He points to one picture and says, "We have trouble with black girls because they don't shave down there," and he points to my pants. "You shave, don't you?"

"Yeah," I say.

"I could tell," he says, "because you come from a good family."

While we're flipping through photos, the wife tells me their story: He was injured in some war and gets disability checks. He can't have sex, so they take photos. The last photo I look at is a woman bent over, with a frying pan in her hand and a spatula up her butt. I tell myself there's no way I'm going to avoid looking pathetic, so I should just get it over with.

The wife says, "I'll help get you ready for him." She motions me into the dining room and shuts the door behind us. She says, "You can undress here, honey." She tells me to sit down, and she puts makeup all over my face—bright blues and dark reds. She pinches my nipples, and she rubs a bright red on the erect part and pale rose on the aureole. "He loves reds," she says, blending the edges of the two colors with her thumb and forefinger. She asks me to stand up, and she combs a comb through my pubic hair. "He'll want it to be soft," she says. She runs the comb, she runs her fingers, and I get shivers, and she says, "OOoohh, isn't that nice?" She rubs her hands up and down my sides. "Try to relax," she says, "he's a very sweet man. Can you relax for him?" I try to relax by pretending I'm not here. I rip my cuticle until it bleeds.

She opens the door, and presents me: "Isn't she beautiful?"

He says, "Yes," and she disappears.

He says he's picked out some clothes, and hands me a shirt with holes for the breasts. It's easy to pose for him because he likes the cheesy stuff; for him, stiff is good.

He gives me shorts with a cut-out crotch, and he is impressed that I can lie on my back on the sofa and do the splits. He calls his wife in to see. She asks me if I can hold that pose or if I'd like her to help. He says I can stay split just fine, and she can go now. He wheels his chair in between my legs and his lens approaches. "Can you put your finger in?" he asks. Then he asks for two, but when he clicks he's out of film. "I'm sorry," he says.

"I'm sorry too," I say.

CAMERON LENDS ME his ball while he's on call, and I spend all week at the beach.

I've seen these three guys every day I've come down. Today they are more desperate than ever, so they ask me to play.

I take a good warm-up. I play with the tall one, and I've watched these guys enough to know that he can't pass the ball and he can't set. All he can do is hit. He says, "Hi, I'm Greg." I introduce myself, and he says, "I see you playing with Cameron a lot. He's a good player. Just set me like you set him."

I want to say, Just pass the ball like Cameron does. I want to say, You know, Cameron gives me half the court.

Greg stands in the middle of the court and steals all the serves that come to me. One serve comes right at me, and I'm so used to giving him the serves that I dodge the ball. He says, "You can take those serves."

We win. The men on the other team scrunch my hand when they shake it. Greg buys me a lemonade and asks if I want to play again. He says he comes down every day at 2:30, and when Cameron's not here, he'd love to play with me. I ask him how he can make a living if he's down here every day at 2:30. He says he's a commodities trader, and the floor is open 7:00 to 2:00.

He says he can get me a job at the Mercantile Exchange. "But you have to play with me after work," he says.

"Okay," I say, "when Cameron's not around."

We pass the ball back and forth while the next team warms up.

"What will I do at the Exchange?"

"You'll be a runner. It's the bottom of the barrel job, but at least you'll get off at two."

"What's a runner?"

"You deliver orders to the pits. You'll see. They'll explain it to you. I'll let you know tomorrow."

The other team comes over to our side of the net, and one of the guys says to me, "We were hoping to play a men's game, so maybe our friend can be the fourth, and you can play on a co-ed net."

Greg doesn't say anything because these guys are better than he is. I want to say, I just won. This is my net now. I want to say, Fuck you. You are so fucking egotistical, and my partner, Cameron, can kick your ass. There is an awkward silence while I'm composing sentences and not saying them.

Greg says, "She usually plays with Cameron. She's not bad," and then we have a game.

MY FAVORITE PLACE to deliver orders is the Eurodollar pit. I don't know what a Eurodollar is, but the pit is huge and busy, and it's all men. The men get excited when I walk by, so when I get a bunch of orders, I deliver them inefficiently so I can walk by the Euro pit and see the men get excited.

The broker I deliver to has three pit clerks. At first, I'd give the order to anyone, but now I know that just one guy holds the pile of orders on paper—the deck—and the other two guys watch for hand signals from the people on the phones—arb.

I walk by the Euro pit on the way to the Swiss pit, and one of the Euro arb guys says, "Hey, you never give me anything anymore."

I say, "That's because you don't hold the deck."

The other Euro arb guy says, "That's not what he's talking about."

I pass by again and the deck guy asks me how I got my legs so strong and tan. I didn't realize my legs were strong and tan. I say, "I play volleyball on the beach every day."

I flex my legs as I walk back to the Bache desk, where I stand around until someone calls in a new order.

I get an S&P order. "Hey," one of the Euro guys yells out, "that slit sure is high."

He's talking about my dress, because I'm the only person on the floor who wears a dress. Actually, it's not a dress but a beach cover-up, and it's slit to the top of my thigh. There are really strict dressing regulations on the floor, and this is one of the only things I own that meets the requirements.

WHEN THE TEMPERATURE is below forty degrees for three weeks, I decide the beach volleyball season is over. I decide to train for a triathlon. I buy three books on triathlons. I learn that triathlons require endurance muscles, and volleyball requires sprinter's muscles, and I don't care.

I do doubles. That's what triathaloners call it: Swim/run, run/bike, bike/swim. I work out for two hours after work and two hours before I go to bed.

THIS GUY catches up with me as I am walking onto the floor. "Hey, do you want to go out for coffee this afternoon?"

"Do I know you?" I ask.

"Well, you walk by me a lot. I stand in between the Swiss pit and the Yen pit."

"How do you know me?"

"Everyone knows the girls on the floor."

He has a red jacket, which means he's a trader, and traders think yellow jackets are scum, so I'm flattered.

He says, "This isn't a date. I'm married."

I say, "Okay."

"I'll meet you in the foyer when the floor closes," he says.

I go downstairs to the lobby, and it looks just like the trading floor but there are no color-coded jackets. I don't see him, so I just stand against a wall, and I hope I look like I have a purpose. I hope I remember what he looks like.

A guy I recognize from the Yen pit comes up to me, "You got a date with MOC?"

"MOC?"

"Yeah. Jimmy Moccio. MOC. That's his badge."

I remember seeing his badge. "Yes."

The guy moves away into the crowd. MOC must have bragged to people in the Yen pit. I like that I'm a commodity.

MOC finds me and we go in his car to a cafe near my apartment. He tells me his car is the result of years of good trading. It's the same car my grandma drives. "It has a car phone," he says. I don't want him to know I'm impressed. I want him to keep trying. He tells me the suburb where he just bought a house. My parents live in a much wealthier suburb.

We get coffee and he tells me about his wife and his kids, and his incurable attraction to me. I put half a cup of milk and three spoon-

fuls of sugar in my coffee and I feel really grown-up having coffee
for socializing instead of late-night cramming.

WHOEVER BECOMES BEST FRIENDS with Jeremy will
get the best pit job. I wear my shortest skirts on days we have
Jeremy's arb class. Jeremy shows us that bid is palm facing in and
offer is palm facing out. I go home and practice in front of the mirror, naked, and in between checking the silouhette of my stomach,
I put my hand up near my face, index finger up: Sell one. This is
how people on the floor will see me.

We learn that you put fingers on your face for the number of lots
bought or sold, and fingers in front of your face for the price. When
it's my turn, I stand on the edge of the pit, where clerks stand, and
Sam pretends he's my broker, and he stands in the pit and yells out
bids and offers. Jeremy pretends he's on the phone talking to some
mutual fund person or something. Jeremy is far away from the pit,
and I flash him the market all the time: 1,2,1,2,1,2,2,3,2,3,2,3,2,3...
Jeremy flashes me orders, and I tell them to Sam. Sam tells me what
price he filled the orders at, and I flash the fill back to Jeremy.

Jeremy makes a motion with his hands like he's breaking a stick
in half.

"What's that?" I yell.

"Break," he says. "I'm asking you if you want to take a break with me."

The whole class is frozen. Sam whispers, "He's asking you on a date."

"Oh," I say, and I yell back, "Okay."

"That's thumbs up," Jeremy says, "don't bother talking on the
floor, no one will hear your voice."

AFTER I'VE DONE THREE MONTHS of triathlon training, my health club has an indoor triathlon that everyone in the health club nags me to enter: "You'll win for sure," the out-of-shape people tell me; "What are you doing all this training for?" the aerobaholics ask me.

I don't do the triathlon. It's a swim/bike day on my schedule, and I turn it into a run/run day so I don't have to go to the health club at all.

I TELL THE EURO GUYS I want to work in the pit. "It's more exciting there," I tell them.

"You should talk to the brokers in the currency pits," the deck holder says. "The Euro pit doesn't have girls."

"That's against the law," I say.

They say I should keep my job for the next few weeks. Christmas is the best time for runners because you get tips from the people you deliver orders to. And girls get the best tips.

For the next two weeks I get tips. Brokers step out of the pit to slip me envelopes with ten-and twenty-dollar bills. I get a $300 tip from a broker in the Swiss pit, and he says he can get me whatever else I want.

"I want a job as a pit clerk," I say.

The next week I have a job in the British Pound pit. I don't know what firm I work for, but I am working with a broker named George, and his clerk, Amy. George's badge is CNT, and everyone calls him Cunt. Amy and I call him George. Amy gives me the deck. She says she's doing arb. I have no idea how the deck is organized, so she explains: The runners bring the orders from the phones to the pit. I file the orders according to the price that activates them. Orders are either above or below the price trading. Every time a runner brings me an order, I file it, or if it's close to the market, I give it to George.

None of the runners knows who I am, so all day they give our orders to other deck holders, and I have to argue with other brokers to get our orders back. The brokers ignore me, until Amy says that the firm we work for will shoot out everyone's fucking windows if they don't give back our orders. I laugh, and Amy says, "Don't laugh. It happened two months ago."

After the close, the Shearson desk manager wants to know if we paid 60 for 10 lots, and George doesn't know what they're talking about. I tell Amy, and Amy says, "Gimme the deck." I hand it to her, and she pulls out an order. "Here," she says. "You filed the Shearson order to buy 10 at 60 with the 80's. Now the market price is 75. So George has to pay 75 for 10, and he has to pay out of his own pocket the extra 15 points on each lot."

"Oh," I say.

"You don't get it, do you?"

"No. Sorry."

"You made a $2,000 error. Don't worry. It's your first day, and people make much bigger errors down here."

THERE'S SOMETHING about Robert Ford that's classier than everyone else on the floor. Maybe it's because everyone calls him his real name instead of his badge letters. Maybe it's because he wears loafers and everyone else wears gym shoes. Maybe it's that he changes his tie—most people leave a tie knotted with their trading jacket in the coat room, and they slip it over their heads every morning. Robert has a fresh tie around his neck every morning. I'm not sure what it is, because he's got blond hair, and I thought I only liked dark, curly, Jewish hair. But I like him.

Yen trading is slow because everyone is watching the fist fight on the far side of the pit. Robert is watching the market. I am watching Robert. If there's any trading going on in the Pound pit, I am missing it.

All the locals want to sell, and the brokers have filled all their buy orders. When someone calls up the Bache desk and says buy 5, Robert sees the arb come into the pit, and before the broker can even say, I'll pay 6 for 5, Robert yells out the broker's name, and hand signals to him sell 5 at 6. Robert gets the trade while the rest of the locals are betting on the fight.

GEORGE IS SHOWING EVERYONE in the pit pictures of his pool, which no one can figure out how he paid for because he makes errors all the time, and he owes a lot of money to the firm we work for. While George is pointing out the monogrammed deck furniture, the Berlin Wall falls down. The pound drops 60 points in six seconds. The whole bottom end of my deck needs filling. Amy tells me to add up how many lots are buys and how many are sells and tell George all at once; George can't deal with a fast market.

There are so many runners bringing me orders that Amy yells out, "We can only take market orders."

A runner asks, "What's the market now?" Amy screams, "No one fucking knows."

I give a rough estimate of buys and sells: "Buy 550, sell 420," I yell to George.

He freezes. It's about five million dollars in trades.

"George!" Amy yells. George doesn't move. "George, MAX is selling 40. Buy 'em. Let's go. You're gonna get hung if you don't get these trades." George doesn't move. So Amy starts buying and selling, and even though she's not allowed to fill orders, all the brokers are trading with her.

Donny has someone on the phone and he's waving frantically. I tell Amy and she says I should take his order. "It's arb," I tell her.

"Like I don't fucking know that," she says.

So I motion for Donny to give me his order, and he flashes me, sell 50 at the market. I make a check mark with my finger in the air: Checking, sell 50 at the market. He is impatient with me for checking such an easy order in such a fast market. "Sell 50," I tell Amy. "50 at 68," she tells me.

I can't believe this is happening. I arb back to Donny: Sold 50 at 68. I am so excited that I forget to give Amy the deck orders coming up. We miss a lot of prices, but Amy says it's okay to fill orders badly in a fast market. Three customers wanted to sell at 74 and we sell them at 45, and Amy says that's fine.

At the end of the day, I have done two hours of arb, and Amy has done two hours of brokering, and George has held four orders in his pocket that he forgot to fill. It cost him $20,000. "Could have been worse than just the Wall," George says, and we all go home grateful.

I BECOME SO GOOD at my triathlon workouts that some days I have enough energy to throw up in between. I decide if I have energy to throw up, then I have energy to train for a marathon, too. I buy *How to Run Your First Marathon*, and I write up a nine-month schedule, which will get me 26 nine-minute miles by October 13, the day of the Chicago Marathon.

MOST TRADERS ARE UGLY because I know they're stupid. I know they're stupid because this place is like a casino without the tuxedos. I try to stick to men in the options pits—you have to be good at math to do options.

The men in the options pits don't give me the time of day. They think I'm an idiot because I'm a clerk in a futures pit, so I bring revealing reading material to work. Today I have *Jane Eyre*.

I park the book at the Shearson desk. The Shearson clerks ask why I'm reading when I'm not in school.

Amy sees the book at the Shearson desk. "Why'd you bring a book to work?"

"I want to read on my break."

"Why don't you talk to people on your break?"

"Because I don't have anything to say."

"George," Amy says, "she's got a book here."

"To read?" George asks.

Amy nods.

George looks at me and says, "The reason you make so many errors is because you read too much. You're not in the real world."

On my break, I take the book to the bathroom. The bathroom is the only place at the Exchange where there's quiet. I start to read, but the book is too slow, and anyway my break is only fifteen minutes. I just sit on the toilet in peace.

On the way back to the floor, Robert, my yen trader, stops me in the hall. "Reading on the job?" he says.

"Just in between," I say.

He says, "I think Jane Austen should write interior decorating books. Her dialogue is flat."

I smile and nod. I have no idea what he's talking about.

When I get back, Amy goes on her break, and I do arb for Donny, who is really high maintenance because he's on the phone five hours a day to a guy in New York. The New York guy compares the price trading in the Pound pit to the price trading among the banks, and when there's a difference he jumps in. So I have to quote the market constantly, which is very difficult because Robert is in the Yen pit now, facing me, and every time I look up, he is looking at me.

"What's the offer?" Donny yells, with his yellow-coated arms flapping in the air. "Hello? Are you with me? What's the offer?"

I flash him three fingers sideways: Eight offer. Then I make a circle over my head: Locals are trading, no brokers, trades are small.

Donny does nothing. I look back at Robert. If I were friends with Robert, I could clerk for him, and then I wouldn't have to be yelled at by someone in a yellow coat. Robert smiles at me.

Donny is waving his arms again. I flash him six bid eight offer, which is my guess at the market, since I've been watching the Yen pit instead of the Pound pit. Donny throws down his phone and stomps down the stairs toward me. "Six bid? Are you kidding me? Eights just traded, and I missed them because you were on another fucking planet. Would you please fucking pay attention? I hope Amy comes back soon."

I look over at Robert to make sure he didn't see me getting yelled at.

SPREAD: To bet above and below the market price, so the trader makes money as long as the market moves.

Common Usage: I'd like to spread that pound chick.

"WHY DON'T YOU wear your wedding ring?" I ask him. "I never would have approached you."

"Well, my marriage isn't going that well."

"I can tell."

"How? You've only known me two minutes."

"Because you were sitting in the pit a half hour after close. Only clerks stay late, not traders. I figure you have a bad life and you don't want to live it, so you sit here."

Robert doesn't say anything. I feel very clever. I say, "This is the most expensive lunch I've had since I moved to Chicago."

"They let me use the phone if I have to call in a trade, so I eat here a lot."

"Well, I'm always available."

"Good."

I don't care that he's married. I don't need to have sex with him. I just want a friend who's a trader. And maybe just a kiss so I know he really wants to be my friend. "We can just be friends," I say. "I need friends because I hate everyone on the floor."

"Why?"

"What do you mean why? Don't you hate them?"

"Yeah, but why do you hate them?"

"Because they're idiots. And all they care about are their pools and their margins."

He smiles.

I decide it's a game: To see how long it takes him to kiss me. To see how irresistible I can be. I want to be so cute and clever that he can't keep his lips off me. I want him to spend lots of time with me. I think I could stop throwing up if I always had him around.

At the museum he wants to be deep, be moved, believe that we're doing something intellectual. I make some comments that I rip off from my art history teacher.

Robert tells me his wife is a docent at the folk art museum across the street. I pretend to be impressed so he can be sure I'm being my cute intellectual self—not trying to get him to kiss me.

He tells me he met her in college, in an art history course and she got the highest grade in the class. "She always got the highest grades," he says.

"She must be smart," I say.

"She just studied a lot," he says. "She's the nicest woman in the world, but she's not an intellectual powerhouse."

I make a note to present myself to him as both—intellectual and nice. On my way to the latter, I say, "She sounds really sweet."

"Yeah," he says, "She's great with our son."

"You have kids?"

"One. And one on the way."

I say, "Do you want to leave now?"

We take a cab back to my apartment, where his car is parked. I want to take cabs for the rest of my life. This is why Robert will be a good friend for me.

I invite him up to my apartment. This will be the first step toward getting a kiss. I think of another step, which will be having him drive me out to my parents' house, since he lives nearby them. I ask him when we get up to my apartment and he says, Yes. I relax because at least I'll be alone with him again on the drive to Wilmette.

He sits down on my floor, and I make popcorn and put the bowl in between us. I eat because I have nothing to say.

He says, "I could never sleep with you unless I loved you."

"And I love my wife," he says. "I mean, I really love her. We have ten years together, and that means a lot."

"Don't worry," I say. "I just want to be friends." When I say this, a kiss seems much more of a challenge.

I look away from him and he lifts my chin with his hand and kisses me. On the lips. With his tongue.

I am mostly disappointed because the game is over.

I kiss him one more time.

DONNY IS TRADING big today. Well, he's trying to, but the first-round games of the NCAA were last weekend, and the Pound pit has a betting pool, and they're discussing who's still in. The Bache clerk waves his hand, he wants to know what's trading. Nothing is trading, and I don't want to bug the brokers for a market quote, so I look up on the board and the last trade was .0035. I tell the Bache guy 1 bid, 9 offer, which is as good as saying nothing's trading. I see him looking around at the other currencies, which are trading heavily; Robert is trading heavily. Donny lodges the phone between his ear and shoulder and throws his arms up in the air in a what's-the-matter shrug. I pantomime dribbling a ball and shooting and he nods. I don't know what he tells the guy on the phone, but they hang up.

When Amy comes back from her break, she tells me Marcy wants to see me in the office.

"Who's Marcy?" I ask.

Amy says, "Just go up there."

I know I'm getting fired, so I get my book from the Shearson desk, and I look for Robert, but I can't find him to say good-bye.

Marcy says, "The bottom line is that you don't take this job seriously enough. Here's a check with three months' severance. You'll have to leave the yellow coat with me."

I walk down eight flights of stairs so I don't have to see anyone in the elevator.

I walk around the edge of The Loop, under the train, trying not to eat things I would want to throw up, trying not to get lost on streets I don't know. I tell myself this is not so bad—I don't have to work again for three months. I am sad because I won't see Robert.

When I get home there are three messages on my machine from Robert. Amy told him what happened and he wonders if I'm okay.

ROBERT MEETS ME for dinner after my first workout in week nine of my marathon schedule. He tells me about the trading floor. "Amy misses you," he says.

"I doubt it," I say.

"MOC asked about you, too."

"How does he know to ask *you*?"

"He saw us looking at each other. Everyone knows. He asked me if we're having an affair, and I said, Yes."

"You did?"

"Yeah. That's what they want to hear."

We take a cab back to my apartment and he wants to come up.

"I still have a swim workout," I say.

"I'd really like to come up," he says. "I'm so attracted to you." He strokes my thighs—the insides. He says, "You have a beautiful body."

I feel my spine tighten, and my vagina gets chills. He didn't touch my thighs last time, so I think maybe he doesn't like Marla anymore. I let him up, and we kiss right away. We sit on my bed and he tells me he loves me, and I tell him we can't have intercourse until he gets a lawyer.

"Okay," he says. "But I'm just dying to kiss your vagina."

"You are?"

"Yes. Has anyone done that for you?"

"No."

"You'll love it. Women love it."

I hope he gets a lawyer soon. "Well, we can't do it tonight."

"Okay. What can we do?"

"Well, let's just start, and I'll let you know."

Robert touches me everywhere, and he's so happy doing it. I say we can take off our clothes, but we have to leave on our underwear. Robert doesn't wear underwear. I think this is very sneaky. I try not to look at his penis.

"I feel sort of funny about this," I say, with both hands on his back.

Robert says he wants to know everything about me. His fingers pry open the lips of my vagina. "Has anyone ever done this to you?" he asks.

"No," I say, and I arch my back.

"What did you do with the guy in college?"

"Intercourse. A lot. Like three times a day."

"Do you like this?" he asks.

I smile.

"Why do you work out so much?" he asks.

It's hard to think of an answer when he's touching me like this. I say the first thing that comes to my head: "For you."

He laughs, and I open my legs a little wider because I can't imagine what he'll do next.

AT PASSOVER, I think about Robert and how good it is that he's married because he's not Jewish. I imagine it being his turn to read at the Passover Seder and the reading is in Hebrew. Tonight everything runs smoothly because we've all gone to Hebrew school.

I go home with my parents for the night because they have better food than I do.

When we pull in the driveway, Robert is sitting on the front steps. Mom and Dad have never seen him but they know. Robert is only ten years younger than my parents. He is almost their equal and he loves me. He looks old when he shakes my parents' hands, and young when he whispers to me that he wants to take me for a drive.

It's good he wants to go somewhere — my dad won't let Robert in the house because he's not Jewish.

When we get in the car, he tells me he left his wife. I want to throw a party, but he's crying. It's easy to be conciliatory when he's in my arms and not hers. He wants to spend the night with me, so we stop by my parents' house and I run in to tell them I'm going back to my apartment.

"He's a nice-looking man," my mom says.

"He left his wife tonight," I say.

"Be careful," she says, and she kisses me good night. "Do you want to take some food back with you?" she asks.

"No," I say, "He'll buy me some."

WE GO TO BERTUCCIONS or Bertallinos, or some expensive trendy Italian place where all the traders go. Robert says the waitress is smiling because she's used to seeing him with his wife. Robert smiles, too. Before we even order wine, a crusty old yen trader comes up to our table and says to Robert, "This must be your wife," like he hasn't met Robert's wife five hundred times.

Robert says, "No, this is my lover." The man walks away, and I feel sexy and daring, and embarrassed for Robert.

ROBERT CRAWLS out of my closet at 5:00 a.m. to go to work. I wake up at 11 a.m., and I have an hour to kill before he's back at my apartment. I move my Judaism books onto the floor to make room for the CD player he brought from home. I cash my unemployment check and buy CDs because he hasn't listened to a new group since Simon and Garfunkel.

When he gets back to my apartment, I'm dancing in the mirror to Sonic Youth. I go over to kiss him but he says I should keep dancing. He wants to watch. I say he should dance with me, but he says he doesn't know how to dance.

"You just do what you want," I say.

"No, I can't," he says.

I dance until the end of the next song. I'm sweaty and breathing heavily, and I pull him into my closet. "I love having you here," I say, and I kiss him and roll onto him and wrinkle his shirt, because now it doesn't matter.

Robert goes to the end of the bed and pulls at the legs of my pants. I lift my hips, and as the pants slip Robert watches my slowly appearing pink.

He takes off his pants. I rub my cheek against the soft blond curls on his leg while he fishes his market computer out of his pants. He tosses it by the pillow. He's short yen, and he has to watch the market.

I move my cheek up his thigh to his balls, and I lick around them and under them because this is what Cameron told me to do during one of my moments of incompetence.

Robert moans and says, "I love this." I put his balls in my mouth and he yells out and drops to his knees. I want to do this forever because I feel like somehow, I got good at it.

He pushes me back on the bed and slips my panties off. He puts them to his face, and I hope they're clean. He licks them and I laugh. He puts his head in between my thighs and says, "Can I kiss you?"

I had been thinking that this is something for after he gets a lawyer, but he's so close, and I'm so curious. "Okay," I say. I spread my thighs a little more, to make room for him, but I don't spread too wide because I want him to think we're doing this for him, not me.

His tongue feels soft and warm. I pick up my head to see what he looks like, and he looks like he's getting really messy. The more he licks around my vagina, the more I want him in there. I hear myself being loud, and the louder I am, the tighter he wraps his arms around my thighs. When my hips are tipped up and my head is tipped back, I'm not even thinking of him when he says, "I want to go inside you."

I'm silent while he adjusts his body so his penis is waiting right outside, waiting for an okay. I am silent while his hips rock his penis back and forth, back and forth, until I say, "Yes."

Afterward, when we're lying together, Robert wants to check where the yen is, but we can't find the computer.

When we sit up, there's a red welt where it dug into my back.

"I can't believe you didn't pull it out from under you," he says, checking the Tokyo exchange.

CAMERON TELLS ME he's engaged and he already has $500 in gifts from Crate&Barrel.

"That's great," I say, and I spend the rest of the day thinking about how much money I could spend at Crate&Barrel if I marry Robert.

I tell Robert I want to go to Crate&Barrel.

I tell Robert if he's really getting a divorce, we may as well register for engagement presents.

Robert glares at me. I register while he roams.

When I'm done, he has a bag of his own stuff. He won't let me peek.

At home, he has me lie down on my kitchen counter, naked, in the dark, and he pulls out of his bag four candles, which he lights. He says I have to guess what he's fucking me with.

The first thing is cold, and when he squirts it, I say, "Whipped cream maker. That was easy."

The next thing is sharp. I guess and guess, and I don't guess right, and he keeps poking me. "Ow," I yell, "ow."

"Do you want me to stop?" he says.

"What is it, and then I'll tell you."

"Do you want me to stop?"

"Ow. It hurts. No. You don't have to stop."

"Good," he says, and then I feel his penis squirming through the whipped cream, soft, with farting sounds when the whipped cream splatters.

I cry, and he leans over the table and kisses my stomach.

The next morning there's a ceramic fondue fork on the floor and a bloody nutcracker in the sink.

THE BABY WAS BORN TODAY, and Robert brought Marla flowers and perfume and wine. He brought me the empty box of Kleenex he went through crying on the drive to my apartment. He is mixed up, he says, and can he call her? I say, Yes, because I want him to think I'm mature enough to understand how much a baby means to a father.

We undress and climb into bed, and I tell him to bend over and spread his cheeks, and he gets hard just from my words, and he gets excited because he thinks this is so racy, and I stick my tongue deep inside him to remind him why he's with me.

I RIDE MY BIKE fifteen miles from the volleyball beach to Wilmette, and I know I'm within fifteen minutes of his house, but I'm lost, with no map, so I call, and Robert picks me up at the drugstore where I used to hang out at the candy counter stealing red hot hearts.

The house is colonial, and he says Marla spends a lot of time decorating. I leave my shoes in the hallway and toss my backpack on the sofa.

Robert takes me to a walk-in closet, where he has one side and Marla has three. He gives me one of his undershirts and a pair of his shorts. "You'll look great in these."

He sits on the toilet while I take a shower. "It took her three hours to get ready for this photo session," he says, holding up her waterproof picture that they keep on the sink.

I get out of the shower, and kiss him lightly while I'm drying myself off. He pushes the towel onto the floor and pulls me onto his lap. He holds my face in his hands. "You have so many large pores," he says, "I wonder what you'd look like if you had enough money to get a facial every week."

I LOVE ROBERT because he has a house and two kids just like my father. He treats his wife like my father treats his. I think Robert and I are soul mates.

Robert loves me because I can sit on his penis and come over and over again, moaning and panting until I pass out. He tells me Marla can't come like I do, with his penis. She needs a finger; she needs someone to teach her how to come, he says. He wants to see her pass out.

I say the right way for a woman to come is with someone who loves her.

He says that's the dumbest thing he's ever heard, because if that were true, his wife would be like me.

I'M LYING in Robert and Marla's bed, which is really Robert's and my bed, because Marla and the kids have abandoned the house. Marla is hanging on all the walls, framed. I sink into her slump in the mattress.

I traipse through the house watching Robert and Marla grow old together. When Marla was my age, she was wide-eyed with a big smile, and always softly-sweatered.

I want to meet Marla. I want to say, Let me show you how to have an orgasm. I want to tip her back and pull down her panties. I want to say, I understand why it's so hard for you to come—it took me three weeks of touching myself every night to figure out how to come. I want to show her how I learned by stroking myself every-where until my body hardened, and then touching the hardest part until it felt good. And I'll help her to make herself shiver—and she'll love me, and she'll love herself, and she'll dump Robert. And then I will dump him too.

CAMERON ASKS ME how Robert is.

I am silent.

"Well, did he leave his wife?"

"Yeah. I'm living with him."

"Where? In your no-bedroom apartment?"

"She moved out of the house," I say. "She moved in with her parents."

"What? She gave him the house to cheat on her?"

"She wants to give him time to think."

"Can he do that?"

I AM READING T.S. ELIOT aloud, and Robert is sighing and smiling. Marla is moving back into the house, so I have to leave after breakfast. He wants to end with teary orgasms and T.S. Eliot on our sheets. He runs his fingers up my spine. They feel like mosquitoes.

ROBERT IS STANDING in front of my building. I can see his shape from a block away. He's not supposed to be here. He's living with his wife and kids. I quickly make up a scenario: Marla told him she's fallen in love with someone else who will support her and the kids; Robert is elated and he's here to give me a huge ring. I compose myself as I approach.

I say to him, "You must be so sad."

He nods and says, "Can I come up?"

While Robert is coming on my quilt and crying on my pillow, the phone starts ringing. Cameron talks into the answering machine: "I know you're screening. Get your lust-worn body out of bed and pick up the phone...Hello?...Hello!...HEL-LO!"

I crawl over to the phone. "What?"

"Is Robert there."

"Yes."

"He's such a loser. How's his wife? Send her my best."

"Can't," I say.

"Oh, now he's reduced you to one-word sentences."

When I hang up, I tell myself Cameron is just jealous. I lean back against the wall, and Robert rests his head on my shoulder until he has to go home.

ROBERT SAYS, "Just one more time," and he comes to pick me up.

After we have sex, I can't sleep.

I tell him I'm going to get some ice cream. Robert asks me to bring a bowl upstairs to share.

In the kitchen, I step on a fork, and it doesn't hurt until I pull it out of my skin, and the skin sticks in between the prongs.

I go upstairs to tell Robert that it hurts too much for me to eat ice cream, and as I'm telling him, a pool of blood is forming at the bottom of the bed.

I am gushing.

Robert wraps a sheet around my foot, but the blood won't stop.

I need six stitches.

We sleep in the guest bedroom.

I HAVEN'T SEEN ROBERT for five days. He's working on fixing things with his wife, but she's not as smart as I am, and Robert needs smart. This is what he told me.

One reason Robert knows I'm smart is because I pick out better books for his three-year-old than she does. I get the books from my grandma's store. I get the artsy ones that have deep adult meaning and cool kid pictures. Grandma makes me pay for the books. I didn't ever have to pay for books before, but I gladly hand over the cash, which I will hit Robert up for later.

Today I buy *Annabel Lee*.

"Where are you getting all this money?" Grandma asks.

I tell her Robert and I are sharing our money. My grandma points out I have no money to share.

When I get back to my apartment, I write an inscription about how our love is as true as the love Poe writes about in *Annabel Lee*, but I don't say that, exactly, because it would be sappy. And instead of inscribing, I write on a notecard, and slip it inside, so he doesn't have to throw out the whole book if he doesn't leave his wife.

CAMERON SAYS he has a present for me. He gives me his three favorite pictures from the Victoria's Secret catalogue. "You can put these up with your pictures of women triathletes," he says.

I examine the pictures. The women all have smooth stomachs with soft belly buttons, and I am pleased. "Thank you," I say, looking at his nose or his forehead—not his eyes, in case I still love them. I say, "There's this part in *I Know Why the Caged Bird Sings* where Maya Angelou says she thought she was a lesbian, but really she was just becoming conscious of her own body and learning to love it."

"So?"

"So, Cameron, how do you think she knows?"

"She's just making excuses. She'd do Toni Morrison if she could."

ROBERT CALLS. He's in his car. He's always in his car when he calls because it's the only phone bill Marla doesn't open.

I haven't seen him for five days because he says that to see me on a day he sees the marriage counselor would be dishonest.

I spend the next half hour preparing for his arrival. I shave my legs twice, once up and down and once diagonally. I place a volleyball and a swimsuit in the middle of the floor so he thinks I've been out playing, instead of home waiting. I've spent all week waiting:

Cleaning behind stuff, putting new stuff in concealed spots, and throwing up.

I sit on my floor and imagine what it will be like when he gets here. He'll look the same as always—khaki pants, brown loafers and oxford-cloth shirt. He wears the same clothes on the weekend that he wears to work. Once I told him his life has no boundaries, and he said he's too old for jeans.

Robert buzzes me and I buzz him back. His eyes dance when they see me, and he kisses me right away, in the door frame; other guys would wait until they walked in and closed the door.

Robert sits down on the floor, which looks funny because we haven't sat anywhere in my apartment besides the bed since the first day he was here. "I have to stop making love to you," he says.

This means he won't be divorcing Marla any time soon. This means my future is disintegrating. I say, "Then why are you here?"

"Because I wanted to tell you in person."

He's told me this in person at least ten times.

"Thank you," I say.

"I can't call you anymore," he says.

"Okay," I say. He's never said this.

We stare at each other. It feels awkward to be clothed. He asks, "What are you going to do now?"

"You mean with my life?"

"Yeah. Are you going to go back to school? Are you going to play volleyball professionally? Are you going to get a job? You're so lucky. The whole world is open to you. You have no responsibilities to anyone but yourself."

"I'm going to try dating women," I say. It comes out quickly and we're both surprised, but I'm relieved to see the lust in his eyes.

"That's great," he says. Then he says, "I have to admit that I'm a little jealous. But I'd sure like to see it."

I can't believe I've gotten myself into this conversation. I know these will be lies that are hard to keep track of: "I have a date this weekend."

"With whom? Do I know her?"

"Robert," I say, "the only women we know in common are the women on the trading floor and your wife."

"Well, I thought maybe it's Amy."

"No, this woman is much more beautiful than Amy."

"Does she look like you?"

"I don't want to talk about it. I'll tell you later."

"But we can't talk later."

"Well, you'll have to use your imagination."

"Okay," he says. "I have to go," he says.

I can't believe he's going to leave without even making out in my bed.

We kiss, and it's passionate, like always, because we always think it's the last time.

I READ ADS all day. I decide looking for men is best in the Wilmette paper because everyone in Wilmette owns a big house. *The Reader* is best for looking for women because it's free, so it attracts the people who are too exciting to hold down jobs.

All the ads sound stupid, so less is best. I answer an ad that says, "five-eight, nice figure, graduate student."

I write a list of things I like. I list stuff like Plato and running and spaghetti so she knows I'm well-rounded. I send her a swimsuit shot, but I don't tell her my dad took it.

After I send my letter, I start worrying that she won't call, and then I binge and throw up.

I go to the bookstore, which is the only safe place for me when I get on the throwing-up track. I spend an hour in the bookstore. I pretend each of the women customers is my ad woman, and I make up scenarios for our first date. One woman is big-breasted and cross-legged on the floor in front of fiction—the M's. We have a great date that ends when I can't figure out a graceful way to get our clothes off.

I realize that for the past hour, I have not thought of Robert once, which makes me even more committed to being a lesbian. I buy *Nice Jewish Girls: An Anthology of Jewish Lesbian Writing* to make sure that being a lesbian will not mess up my life.

CAMERON COMES DOWN to the beach and I'm playing on a woman's net. He sits down to watch.

"You're getting good," he says.

"Thanks."

"How have you been?"

"I'm okay when I'm playing, but when I go back to my apartment, all I do is think about Robert."

"Why don't you come to a movie with me and Julie tonight?"

"Doesn't she hate me?"

"No, not at all."

I go out of curiosity, mostly. Julie is short and Asian and I have a better body. Cameron has a thing for Asian women. She feels superior because she got Cameron. I feel superior because she's ugly. We are very nice to each other.

We see *Fatal Attraction*, and I cry at the end when the man goes back to his wife.

HER NAME IS PATTI, and she calls three days later. I say I'm glad she called. I want to ask what sorts of replies she got, but I don't want to seem insecure. She suggests dinner and we pick a time. I tell her I'll pick her up; I want to be in control.

I beg to borrow my parents' car. I have to have it back by midnight, but that might be good if she turns out to be ugly.

As I pull up to her apartment, I rewind the tape to "Sweet Virginia" because it sounds erotic but not obviously erotic. She must be loaded because her apartment building is full of marble. I ring her bell and she makes me wait five minutes in front of fifty mirrors, and when she comes down, every one of my six thousand hairs is in perfect place, which is good because all of hers are too. She could be a model. She has large breasts and long legs. I hope she thinks I'm beautiful, too, but I feel big and gawky, so I try to make up for it by being suave and confident. She says, "Hi," and I shake her hand. As we walk to the car, she presses her lips together to keep from smiling. I let my arms swing and my keys jingle.

"Sweet Virginia" starts up, and I ask her if she has an idea of where to go. She has no ideas, so we drive around until we spot an upscale pizza place.

This is what I tell her about myself: I am planning to play professional beach volleyball. I used to work on the trading floor.

This is what I find out about her: She's planning to be a nurse anesthesiologist. She used to be a professional ballerina.

CAMERON AND I are warming up. When we hit at each other, we pass the ball up perfectly, until he says, "I'm cheating on Julie." I am glad to hear he didn't reserve all his cheating for when he was with me.

"Aren't you engaged?"

He catches the ball. "Yeah. But I panicked that I would never have sex with anyone but Julie for the rest of my life."

"Who is it?"

"Pearl. You don't know her. She's sixteen. She's a secretary in the ER."

"Sounds like you two are really compatible."

"She has a golden tongue."

"Why is it golden?" I want to know if mine is golden.

"Last night, she said, 'I want you to come in my mouth.'"

I let Robert come in my mouth all the time, so I have a golden tongue, too. I can't believe Julie left a message about blow jobs if she doesn't have a golden tongue. I'm embarrassed for her.

I hit the ball hard at Cameron, while he's thinking about Pearl. Or Julie. It doesn't matter.

PATTI AND I work out at her expensive health club. We run twenty laps and swim fifteen. I am in much better shape than she is. I don't tell her that I work out three times a day to keep myself from bingeing and thinking about Robert. She says she feels like an unworthy running partner. I like that. When we go to the locker room, I wonder if we should go in separate rows. We don't talk about it, though. We undress next to each other.

This is what I tell her about me: I am attracted to the women I play volleyball with. I just got dumped by a married man.

This is what I find out about her: She was attracted to the other women dancers in her company. She just dumped a doctor who was supporting her in her own apartment.

I TELL HER I don't really have a car, so she always has to drive. She wants to dance. She wants to check out the lesbian club scene. We go to one, and it's full of industrial lesbians drinking beer and wearing sneakers. The next one we go to has flashing lights on the outside and dancing women on the inside. We watch for a little, to see how women do it. They seem to be doing it just like men and women do it; you dance like you're by yourself.

I start sweating after about four songs, and I don't want to be sweaty, in case this is the night Patti sleeps over, so we stand on the side for a while. Three different women ask me to dance. I say No to all of them. I say I'm with Patti.

Men never approach me like this. I decide I'm a much hotter commodity among lesbians. I could have more power if I stuck to women.

This is what I tell Patti about myself: I want to be a writer, but I have never written anything. I'm bulemic. Well, I say I used to be.

This is what she tells me about herself: She's had plastic surgery three times. She's a hooker. Used to be.

ROBERT CALLS and he says he has to see me.

I don't want to see him. I don't love him. He's too fucked-up.

"What time?" I ask.

"Seven," he says. And I know Marla moved out again, or he'd have to come over during the day.

I call Patti when I know she'll be at school, and I leave a message that we'll have to reschedule. "Something suddenly came up," I say.

He comes over with a bottle of wine and no explanations. I don't ask. I just drink his wine, and we get into bed quickly, before we have to talk about anything prickly, which is everything.

He kisses my vagina, and it feels good if I don't think about who's doing it. I'm not on the pill anymore, so I tell him to come in my mouth. He's rolling his hips and stroking my hair. He tells me he loves me, and I am glad my mouth is full.

PATTI PICKS ME UP. She wants to go to another lesbian club.

I say, "I think we know each other well enough to kiss. Are we ever going to kiss?"

Patti looks straight ahead, over the steering wheel. She presses her lips together so she doesn't smile.

"Let's just wait until it happens," she says.

"It's not going to happen if we don't make it happen. I'm getting antsy."

"Okay," she says, and she turns her face to me. I lean toward her and kiss her. I put my hands on the back of her head and she puts her hands on the steering wheel.

We kiss for about a minute. Enough for me to say I know what it's like to kiss a woman, but not enough to call myself a lesbian. I have a huge smile on my face. "Thanks," I say, "that was really nice." I know it means a lot to her to kiss me because she doesn't kiss tricks, and she doesn't let the doctor use his tongue.

We go to the club.

This is what I tell her about myself: I love her legs.

This is what she tells me about herself: Three of Robert's friends in the Yen pit were her clients.

I TELL HER to park her car and come up to my apartment. She likes coming up because she likes my books. "You have such a curious mind," she says.

"Let's have sex tonight," I say.

"I have to be in the mood," Patti says.

"Well, what do you need?"

"I need to be in control. I'm used to being the one in control." I lie down on the floor. "Okay. You take control."

She says, "I don't know what to do."

"Let's take off our clothes and get in bed."

"Let's leave on our underwear," she says.

We both have on lacy black panties. We lie down side by side, facing each other, and I put my hand on her breast—the top one. Her skin feels good.

"I feel stupid," she says.

I feel stupid too, but I want to feel her body against mine. I want to know what it's like for breasts to come together. I say, "Just try it," and I put my face close to hers, and she laughs. And then I hate her.

"Let's get dressed," I say.

"Are you sure?" she says. "Are you angry?"

"No, I'm not angry," I say, throwing her clothes at her. I pull my T-shirt over my head.

She leaves.

I TELL MY MOM I'm a lesbian now, and I'm bringing my girl-friend home for dinner. Mom says, "Does this woman like dark meat or white?"

"What? Mom, aren't you surprised?"

"No. You've always had a lot of trouble with men."

I say, "Forget it. I just decided I'd rather come alone."

I tell Patti I don't want to see her anymore. I give no explanation, and she doesn't ask.

I JUST FINISHED sitting at the mahogany dining room table. Now I'm sitting at the stark white kitchen table. I move between the two for variety. I am annoying my mother while she cooks lunch, hoping the day will go faster.

"You're going to have to stop waiting for him," my mom says. "It's dragging your whole life down."

"I don't have a life."

"Well it's dragging your volleyball down."

"Wow," I say. "You're worried about my game?"

"He's not as great a guy as you think. If he'd cheat on his wife, he'd cheat on you."

"He loves me, Mom. I know he loves me."

"He could love you and still never be able to leave his family, and you have to accept that."

I move back to the dining room. I know I should not want to get back together. I know I'm wasting brain cells planning our future. But it's so hard to plan my future without him. It's hard to draw all new pictures. It's so much easier to start with a picture of his house, or his restaurant, or his hair.

I GO TO a lesbian bulemic overeater's anonymous meeting to get picked up. At the meeting all the women are beautiful, except for one really fat woman who is a sex addict left over from the group that meets right before this one.

We go around the room and say our names and that we are

bulemic. I hate saying it, and I tell myself that I am not bulemic. I am not like these women. I am done throwing up.

I don't listen to anyone sharing. I pick out two women in the meeting and I tell myself that I must ask one of them out. I'm nervous, but if I make an ass of myself, I can go to a different meeting.

The first woman who introduces herself to me asks if I want to get coffee.

Her name is Rachel, and she's Jewish, which means she's the first date in years who would meet my family's requirements.

She takes me back to her apartment and shows me personal, meaningful things. I try to be interested and compassionate, but I don't want her to think this is long-term. She says she hasn't thrown up for two years. I tell her I don't throw up anymore, either. While she talks to me, I size her up—not gorgeous, but an incredible voice. She's got a flat stomach but flat breasts. I hope for really big nipples.

ROBERT IS LIVING alone at his house, fixing things. He calls me up to ask if I want to have lunch. "It's a beautiful day," he says. "So you're probably going to play volleyball."

"Yeah," I say, "I do want to play volleyball." He's silent. "Do you want to come with me?" I say.

"That would be nice."

"Come quickly. If I get there too late, all the nets will be filled."

He picks me up in a new BMW. "You bought a car?"

"Yeah. Do you like it? It has a CD player. Listen." He presses play and L.L. Cool J comes on.

"You bought that?" I ask.

"Yeah. I thought you said it was good."

"Well, good if you're going to live with me."

"I like it," he says.

"This car is an extension of your midlife crisis. This is like when my dad bought a motorcycle."

"This is not a midlife crisis. It's deeper than that."

At the beach he gets a Nieman Marcus beach chair out of the trunk and he folds the *Wall Street Journal* under his arm. He's wearing khaki pants.

We walk to the courts, and I get ahead of him in the sand. You can tell a volleyball player by the way she walks through the sand—upright and steady. Robert wobbles and doesn't pick his feet up high enough. I wait for him, but once I'm on the beach I'm anxious to get a game. "Sit here," I tell him.

Before I find a court to challenge, some guy asks me to play. He says, "You can have half the court," because he knows I hate playing co-ed.

"Okay," I say, and head over to the court. I leave Robert in the sun with no lotion and a paper that's already turning yellow.

RACHEL TAKES ME dancing to introduce me to the lesbian club scene. It's different from going with Patti, because Rachel has friends here. I hope Rachel and I will have sex tonight because I don't want to have to be this social again.

She walks me back to my apartment, and I invite her up, and when we get there I feel awkward standing in the middle of the apartment, so I force myself to kiss her. After a couple of seconds, it feels good, and I decide I should kiss her like I'd kiss a man because then I'll know what to do. Our tongues slide together and my hands run up and down her body.

We move to my bed, and I try to take off her shirt. I want to get everything off as fast as I can.

"No," she says. "I like to keep our clothes on as long as possible."
I don't tell her I'm already at my limit. I leave her shirt on and put
my hand under. I want to feel every part of her.

Once I realize that we really are going to have sex, I tell myself
that I can go slower.

I want to see what I'm touching, so I get out of bed and turn on
the bathroom light.

I can't keep my hands still. Everything is so soft and smooth, and
I can't believe how much freedom my hands have with her body. It
doesn't feel real. I feel like I'm doing something sneaky, unofficial,
outside of any rules.

The next time I push her shirt up, she helps it over her head. I
take off her bra, and I feel like I'm playing dress-up. Before she can
move, I take off all my clothes. I want to feel my body against hers.

I move my hands across her breasts a million times before I put
my lips to them, because I still feel sort of funny. But once I do it I
can't stop.

For a while, I don't notice what she's actually doing. "Tell me
what to do," I say, in case she forgot that I have no experience doing
this. She tells me to turn over. "Why?" I ask.

"It's better on your stomach. Did you know that? It's more intense
that way." I want to believe she knows everything in the world about
lesbian sex, so I turn over and spread my legs. My back is arched,
and I rise up a little on my knees and rest my head on my arms, and
before she even touches me, this position feels good. I can't tell
what she's doing—if she's using her fingers or her mouth. She's not
soft like Robert—she's hard and rhythmic. I am loud, because
Robert likes that, but I stop to say, "Wait, show me what you're
doing." She says she has three fingers in me.

"Three?"

"Yeah," she says, "you seem to like it."

I do like it, but now I want to do it to her. So I arch my back a lot and squeeze my muscles, and I come. Usually, I'd want to come again, right away, but I want to do it to her.

"Okay," I say, "you lie on your stomach." She lies down and spreads her legs. "Rachel, I can't see anything. How about if you start on your back."

She flips over, and she puts her arms behind her head so her back arches a little. Her breasts are flat and her stomach is flat, and everything seems to slope to her thighs. I rub my face in her pubic hair, and it smells a little salty and a little musty and I take deep breaths until I know her scent. I spread the lips of her vagina, and her clitoris is huge. I lift my face and rest my chin in her hair. "Rachel, do I have an undersized clitoris?"

She says, "Well, it's smaller than mine. But I've seen smaller."

I spread her lips again, I hold them open and run my tongue softly up and down. I make circles, and I suck, and I kiss. She says, "Yes," sometimes, so I can tell how I'm doing.

"Bite," she says.

I take little bites on the side, and she spreads her thighs wider, and she rocks her hips, and I get so excited that I bite where I should be licking, and Rachel yells out.

"Sorry," I say. "I'm really sorry."

She pulls me up by the arms to her mouth. "You have to wait a minute," she says, "that really hurt." She kisses me like it's okay that I just took a bite out of her, and I love her for being so forgiving. Our mouths taste salty and musty, and my legs are wrapped around her waist, tightly. I want to be inside her. I stick my tongue deep in her mouth. I stick my tongue in her ear and she giggles. I stick my tongue in her vagina slowly, and she moans. She turns over, and she says, "Use your fingers."

I put three in and out and she moves her hips with me. She says, "You can put in more than three."

I wonder how she can tell how many I'm using. I put in four, and my hand glides in and out. I push harder and harder. I love making her scream with each thrust.

She drops her hips and my hand slips out, and then I can tell that she's come. I feel a little silly for not knowing when it happened, but I'm really proud that I made her come.

I crawl up her back, and I lay my wet hair on her warm butt. I put my arms over hers and I kiss the back of her neck. I kiss behind her ears, and I whisper, "More."

I fall asleep with my face in her thighs, but she wakes me up when she flips over. She puts her face next to mine and kisses me good night.

She sleeps. I can't sleep with her face right there, so I think. I think it was fun to do this, but I don't want to have to talk to her when she wakes up.

I don't want to go down to the newspaper stand holding hands.

I think about how everything we did was for an orgasm, and if we're just going to put stuff in each others' vaginas we should just use penises. I am relieved to know that I like penises better than women. I feel self-righteous that I tried sex with a woman and didn't like it.

I want her out of my bed. I want to try masturbating on my stomach.

I want to throw up, and I would have to lie to her if I don't get rid of her.

"HI. IT'S CAMERON. What's up?"

"I'm packing."

"Where are you going?"

"I'm moving to Los Angeles."

"What? When? How can you just be telling me now?"

"I just decided. There's no reason to stay here. I'm better than all the women and the men won't play with me."

"Your defense sucks."

"I know. I'm working on it. I'm going to live with my parents and save my unemployment checks, and I'm moving in March."

"Well, we'll have to play a lot before you go. I want to be able to say I played with a pro beach volleyball player."

I'M LIVING in my parents' attic and I'm working on my defense.

I don't talk to my parents except to borrow the car. They hate that I treat their house like a hotel, but they love that I'm planning to move away from Robert.

Every morning, my mom drives me and my dad to the train, and he gets off at his office and I get off at the beach.

The key to defense is believing in yourself—relaxing, and knowing that wherever the person puts the ball, you can get there. But it's not enough for me anymore to just touch the ball. I have to get it up where I want it on the court; no one will give me a good set if I can't pass the ball where I want it.

DAD HAS TO CARRY my suitcases because wheeling my
bicycle through O'Hare is all I can manage. The baggage check
clerk won't accept my bike as it is, so I snap off the tire and my dad
removes the pedals.

Once my stuff is checked, we walk two miles through the United
terminal's moving sidewalk/electric light show and then we wait at
the gate. Dad gives me a pep talk: I can call collect, there's a big
Jewish community in Los Angeles, I can always come back to
Illinois.

As I get up to leave, he asks me if I want to take any of his money,
and I look at the floor and say, "Yeah. That would be nice."

He puts his credit card in my hand and a kiss on my cheek, and
I board the plane to L.A.

THE TRUCKER SAYS he'll arrive on Wednesday or Thursday.
I sit in my apartment waiting, and leave only to binge on Thursday
morning.

He arrives late Thursday.

I unpack the books and organize them by subject, and then by the order I've read them. I worry about whether Nice Jewish Girls goes in the lesbian section or the Jewish section. I put it with the Bibles.

I spend four days trying to figure out how to attach the shelves to the walls so the books don't kill me in an earthquake.

On the fifth day, I give up. I put the heavy books on the bottom and the light books on top, and I go play volleyball.

MY UNEMPLOYMENT RAN OUT the week before I left for L.A. My dad's Visa card doesn't work because it has his signature on the back. I had some money saved, but it's gone because when I binge, no food is too expensive.

I wait until I've lived for two days on six bagels, and then I am hungry enough to get a job at Crate&Barrel—lining up glasses and dishes so that it looks like the Gap. This job is beneath me, but I tell myself it's part of being a professional volleyball player—I can't have a real job because I can only work at night.

My first week there, the manager tells me she's sorry, but I have to work next Monday night.

"Don't I work every Monday?" I ask.

"Yes, you do, but this Monday is the Oscars, and I just want you to know we don't close."

"Oh," I say.

On Oscar night, it's just me and the assistant manager—not one customer the whole evening.

I tell her I came to L.A. to play professional beach volleyball.

She tells me she has a degree in anthropology and she doesn't know what to do with her life, and she's scared.

I feel sorry for her.

MOM CALLS to see how I'm doing. I tell her I'm playing a lot of volleyball.

"When are you going to figure out what you want?" she asks. "It's such a shame to see you starting over in California with no sense of priority."

"I am trying to get into the pro circuit."

"I think you're kidding yourself."

"You don't understand anything but academic ambition."

"If you had any ambition, I'd be happy."

"Mom, you don't understand."

"I wish that were true. My heart really breaks for you, honey. Have you thought about cash? How will you live? You can't live off minimum wage."

This means she will not be giving me any money. "I don't need a lot."

"You need more than you think."

I NEED TO ORGANIZE my life to reflect my priorities. I need to focus. I make a schedule:

8:00–8:15   Walk to bagel shop.

8:15–9:15   Eat ten bagels and coffee.

9:15–9:30   Walk home.

(9:30–9:45	Throw up completely. Eat one handful of vomit for energy.)
9:45–10:00	Dress for the beach.
10:00–10:30	Ride bike to the beach.
10:30–4:00	Volleyball.
4:00–4:30	Ride home.
4:30–5:00	Shower.
5:00–5:30	Buy four bagels. Bring them home. No eating until I get home. No throwing up.
5:30–10:30	Work. Or read.
10:30	Bed.

I NEED TO GET MONEY. So I call Cameron:

Me:	Hi, it's me. Can I have some money?
Cameron:	For what? Are you okay?
Me:	I'm fine. My parents are being assholes. My mom just called to tell me I'm a loser.
Cameron:	How's volleyball?

Me: It's good.

Cameron: How much?

Me: I can't pay you back. I mean, I don't know when.

Cameron: It's okay. Last week, I blew off Julie and took a
               patient out for a $200 dinner. Giving you my
               money will be good for my marriage.

Me: Did you kiss that woman?

Cameron: Yes, but not in public, out of respect for Julie.

Me: Wow, that was really respectful.
Cameron: I knew you'd think so.

Me: How about $300?

Cameron: I'll send you $500 .

IT'S RAINING and I'm excited. This is the first time it's rained
since I moved to L.A. , and I need a day without volleyball. I spend
the day reading and watching the street flood outside my window. I
walk to the bagel shop past tons of skidding cars because no one
here knows how to drive in the rain. The bagel shop man compliments me on my rain shoes: "That's a really clever idea," he says.

I am proud that everyone else's feet are wet, and mine are staying dry. But then I realize that I am the only person walking in the
rain because everyone else in L.A. has a car.

MY INCOME: Ninety percent goes to rent. After that, I don't have food money, and when I do get money, I eat everything in sight.

I tell myself this no-money situation will be good for me because there won't be anything to vomit. But the larger problem is that I don't have money for medicine and my athlete's foot is spreading from my skin to my toenails.

I begin supplementing my income by swiping stuff and selling it to volleyball players at discount prices. I discover that Crate&Barrel sells the same aprons as Bed, Bath & Beyond, and Bed, Bath & Beyond sells books, and Waldenbooks gives cash back without a receipt, as long as they carry the merchandise. So for a while, I do this: I steal four aprons, and one apron is good for two copies of *Where The Wild Things Are*, which gets me twenty-seven dollars cash from Waldenbooks.

MY MOM CALLS. She says a cousin I never met is having a wedding in Pasadena, and Mom and Dad are flying in for it.

I say I'll go, but I won't stay in the hotel with them.

"How will you get to Pasadena?" my mom asks.

"Oh yeah," I say, "I guess you'll have to pick me up."

Mom sends me a check to buy a dress. I look on my map for a familiar department store, and I ride my bike to Lord&Taylor, but the distances are much further than my map shows, and by the time I get there I'm too sweaty, so I go back home.

I use the money to buy two hundred bagels that I freeze, and toilet paper so I can stop using dirty T-shirts.

AT SOME POINT you have to get out of the context of the game to make yourself play better. But the only drill I can do is jump serving because I'm scared to ask anyone to drill with me. I'm scared they'll think I'm not good enough.

I do 100 jump serves a day. I like the rhythm—the same toss, the same three steps, the same swing, every time. I get an inconsistently spinning, very fast serve, that most players can't return. But the serve is only one part of the game, and I'm not sure what to do to improve the rest, and I know I need someone to help me.

I LET THE PHONE RING because I can't think of anyone I want to talk to. But this time it's relentless, so I pick it up. It's Robert.

He says he's playing golf. In Arizona. He wants me to sleep over.

I brag to the Crate&Barrel workers that the most prominent yen futures trader in the United States is flying me to Arizona.

The manager asks if I can do the flatware when I get back.

I leave right after my shift. I take a cab to the airport because he's paying.

I arrive in Scottsdale at 11 p.m.

We smile. We hug. We kiss, and it's an effort to keep my tongue out from in between his teeth.

He says I look great. I smile. He looks fat.

He gives me a tour in the dark. Lots of cacti and lots of ranch houses—everything in Scottsdale lies low. "This place is great for my game," he says, pulling up next to his golf course.

His hotel room has a king-size bed, and a bottle of champagne. His suitcase has three kinds of condoms.

"Everything's set," he says. He looks at me and he can tell in my eyes that I am not. He kisses me so that he's too close to see my eyes without going cross-eyed.

I know I'm never going to like this. I know if I tell him he is a pathetic, cheating, selfish man, I would risk his not paying me back for the plane tickets and cab rides. So I kiss back, and I try to like it, because he won't like it if I don't. I moan and squirm, but I feel like an idiot. So I say, "Robert, undress yourself."

"Okay," he says. He fumbles with buttons. He asks, "Are you undressing, too?"

"No," I say, "I'm sitting in this chair and watching."

"Okay," he says. He loves it when we do new things. In fact, he loves me because we do new things. In fact, he doesn't love me.

I hate him.

I run my fingers like spiders down his back and down his butt, and when I get to the backs of his knees, he buckles. "Don't move," I tell him. And he lets out a deep sigh and gets hard.

I run my fingers down again, and he's still. "Good," I tell him.

I want to bend him over and ram the champagne bottle up his ass. This is why I hate him—because that's what he wants from me.

I give him a blow job. He's so used to his wife not letting him come in her mouth that he pulls out midstream and gets it all over my face.

We crawl into bed, and I say I'm very sleepy and he says he wants to make me come. I roll over on my back and spread my legs. He wants to use his mouth, but I don't want him that close to me, so I tell him I've been dreaming of his fingers. He puts a few inside me, and right away, I yell and scream and jerk my body, and I say, "I forgot how intense it is with you."

I think this will satisfy him, and we can go to sleep, but he wants to touch more. He wants to cuddle. He wants me to come more. He wants me to play with his balls. I'm very tired of what Robert wants. I let him put his fingers in me one more time before we go to bed.

HEIDI AND I are warming up.

Heidi says, "Are you going to warm up or stare at the ocean?"

"I'm trying," I say.

She says, "Forget it. Let's go for a walk."

The other players are relieved because last time Heidi played, she switched the ball three times, and accused the other team of cheating twice—which they did—but no one would say it as undiplomatically as Heidi. I don't want to be alone with her. "I can't take a walk," I say. "I have to go home."

"You don't have to go home," she says. "You were about to stay here and play another game."

We run at a slow pace in the soft sand on a beach that goes for miles.

Once she has me a safe distance from everyone, she says, "Are you an addict?"

"What?"

"You have this special combination of a hidden life and visibly erratic behavior."

"And that equals drugs?"

"Yeah. It does. Look, I know the behavior of an addict, and you have it."

"I don't use drugs. They scare me."

"Well," Heidi says, "I like you."

"You do?"

"Yeah. I can see you feel a lot, and I like that. You look sad."

I say, "I got fired from my job yesterday. It's a stupid job. Just clerical. But I'm scared that I won't have enough money."

"Fired for stealing?"

"How did you know?"

"All clerical workers steal or else they starve."

I don't say anything because I don't want her to think she's my friend.

And besides, we're back at the nets. We exchange phone numbers and I am embarrassed that other people are seeing me be friends with Heidi.

WALDENBOOKS has no alarm system and very tall shelves. I can't go in too often, or for too long, so I have to have organized reading lists. I started out with the nineteenth-century D's: Dostoyevsky, Dumas, Dreiser, Dickens, and George Sand because she was misshelved. I did K's and P's because those sections are hard to see from the counter. Then I noticed philosophy is a real cinch, so I stole *The History of Philosophy*. I made a list of deconstructionist philosophers, and I stole them. From the footnotes, I did a list of French feminists, but Waldenbooks doesn't have very many, so I special-ordered Cixous and Irigary, and I paid for them by exchanging books on Judaism that my dad sent to me.

Today I'm stealing books that are on my feminist psychology list. Two of the men on the staff are staring at me, so I pay cash for *Women and Madness* to throw them off.

▼

I TRY NOT TO PLAY a lot of games with Heidi because she's not serious about playing and I want to get a good partner, but all the other nets are filled with players I've never met.

While we're waiting for the other team to warm up, Heidi tells me she works as a personal secretary for movie stars.

"Which ones?" I ask.

"Esther Williams," she says.

She got the job from Esther's podiatrist, who used to be Heidi's dealer.

Esther pays Heidi $25 an hour to do stuff like buy swimming pool filters and pick up videos from the Academy for screening. Esther is looking for someone to answer her fan mail for seven dollars an hour. Heidi won't go that low.

I tell Heidi I'll answer Esther's mail.

On my bike ride home, I stop for bagels and only eat two.

I GO TO A CAFE to meet men who read something besides Volleyball Monthly. At the cafe there's a guy whose name is Tohonee, and he's at a microphone reading his poems. The first one he reads is from the woman's perspective about this guy in an arcade who starts out playing video games and ends up raping a girl in the back room. Tohonee explains the rape like a gruesome video game adventure. Tohonee is delineating the impact of video games on the postmodern male. On top of that, he exudes a men's movement sensitivity to speak from a woman's mind.

I order a glass of wine in between the poems so that I'm buzzed enough to approach this god-of-all-liberated-males after the reading.

He makes an announcement that all the proceeds from his newest book will go toward a battered women's shelter. Then he reads more poems about battering women.

After he reads, the audience swarms over him. I stay in my seat. I try to remember what Andrea Dworkin wrote about Henry Miller's stories but nothing applicable comes to mind.

By the time the crowd has disintegrated, I have some things to says to Tohonee, so I go up to him. "You act like a fucking savior of all women," I tell him. "Your poems are such a crock." He looks at me. "I see you getting a hard-on while you read—I know these are your fantasies."

"So?" he says.

I realize I'm blushing, and Tohonee is smiling. The silence is on the brink of awkwardness, and because he's an asshole, he's not helping me out.

He strokes my cheek, which is audacious of him, but it feels good. There's something really erotic about a tender touch from a violent man.

I go home with him.

We drive in his car and say nothing to each other the whole way there. I'm nervous and giddy, and excited with the thrill of not knowing what will happen.

In his apartment he makes us drinks and then pushes me against the wall with a kiss. "So you want to act out fantasies," he says.

Even though it's not a question, I answer, Yes.

"You sure?" he asks, with a very serious look in his eyes.

"Yeah," I say. But he's looking at me like one of the characters in his poems, or one of the characters in my fantasies, and he looks like he could kill me. "No cuts or burns," I say. "I want this to be over in one night. I don't want to be in the hospital or anything."

"Oh," he says, "So you want to be in charge? Then you better stick to your own fantasies and I'll drive you home."

I SAY YES to Laura, because she has a reputation for knowing what to do and not being able to do it—she will be a partner who gives me good coaching. I also say Yes to Laura because she's a lesbian. There are lots of lesbians on the tour who would be beautiful to lie right next to, legs intertwined. Laura is not one of them, but Laura is smart, and I want to philosophize.

Laura says I should work on my cut shot because if I can't go short cross court, it's too easy to play defense against me. Laura works on deep hits to far corners. A cut shot is much harder to hit; I decide that I'm a better hitter so I can ask questions about her personal life and she won't dump me.

I ask Laura how she knew she was a lesbian.

She says she just did, "For as long as I can remember." She says I should swing harder on the cut.

I swing harder and I tell her I am thinking maybe I am a lesbian. Laura says, "Oh."

I tell myself that she is coaching me and that's what I want, and I should stop thinking about everything else.

HEIDI AND I are eating at the Bagel Nosh, which is one of my sponsors. Since I eat for free here, I usually binge here, so no one notices when I fill up my tray with enough food for Heidi and me.

Heidi has someone for me to go out with. He's a friend of a friend of Esther's accountant.

I tell Heidi I'm not going.

"You're being an idiot," she says. "We're not talking adolescent volleyball players here. This guy's a computer wiz kid. He's got nice friends and a 1969 Porsche."

"I just want to play volleyball and read."

"You are so full of shit."

"I can't handle anyone in my life. I need time to throw up. I need time to tweeze. What did you tell him about me? Did you say I'm a volleyball player?"

"Yeah."

"I bet that really impressed him."

"It did. It impresses everyone who knows nothing about it. Will you get some more cole slaw, in one of those to-go containers?"

"Heidi, you already have three to-go containers."

"It's free. Just get one more."

I get it and sit back down. Heidi says, "You're not eating."

"I know," I say. "I would never binge in someone else's company."

"There's another reason to go out with this Andy guy."

"He'll think I'm an idiot, or he'll think I'm smart and pissing my life away at the beach."

"He's calling you tonight. If you say no, you'll be losing a great opportunity. This guy could really take care of you. Will you get me some bagels, sliced?"

"This is it, okay, Heidi?"

"Okay, thanks. And none of those annoying black seeds."

IT'S A LAXATIVE DAY. I can't move because I'm scared I'll shit in my pants. I'm dead tired, because I started waking up to shit at about 5 a.m., and it hasn't stopped. Actually, shitting isn't an accurate term because it's so watery. I hope that my body is drained before I have to leave for my cousin's wedding.

I tell myself this doesn't count. I tell myself I never would have eaten food that I can't throw up if I hadn't been out to dinner with my parents last night. I tell myself I wouldn't have to be thin today if I didn't have to show my parents that I'm in great shape from working so hard at volleyball.

It takes me three hours because I have two accidents, which require showers because the shit is dripping down the backs of my thighs; it's really difficult to control liquid with the sphincter muscles.

My parents pick me up late and they talk about graduate programs in history for next fall. My dad thinks he can get me into Yale.

I arrive at the wedding in a blissful state of starvation and dehydration: Definitely a few pounds lighter from the laxatives.

My cousin has on a white gown with a ten-foot-long train, a two-layered veil, and a Victorian collar. She looks like a Madame Alexander doll.

After the ceremony, a band starts playing. I mean, one of the bands. There's a band for each mood section of the party, according to her mother, the woman who made a career out of throwing this wedding. I'm looking for the bad mood band, and also for the bathroom in case I'm leaking. I put a maxi pad in to catch the drips.

My parents eat and I do not. My parents dance and I do not. I take an hour-long walk around historic Pasadena and hit all the significant bathrooms.

On the drive back to Santa Monica, I think about my wedding, which is surely down the road, somewhere, and I try to imagine myself in a wedding dress. But the only thing I see down my road is a huge wedding cake, right in the middle, going in my mouth one minute, and coming out as shit the next.

HEIDI DROPS OFF 100 three by five head shots.

"three by five's? No one will want these," I say.

"I know," she says. "Esther wants you to send these to people who don't provide return postage."

ANDY HAS PORK which makes me sick, but we won't kiss tonight, anyway.

I panic that bagels are not on the menu. I have spaghetti and I swear to myself that I'll only eat half so I won't throw it up.

He asks me what I do.

I say I play professional beach volleyball, and I am grateful that I have an answer to the question.

After dinner he wants to see my apartment. He says Heidi told him he'd learn a lot about me from my apartment.

I say no. The only thing he would learn is that my books are my life and they are very unorganized because I'm scared they're going to fall on me.

VOLLEYBALL PARTNERS are like sex partners: You click or you don't; you communicate, or you don't. Laura doesn't feel funny telling me where she wants her set—even if I'm only a little off the mark. And when I give her a great set, and she crushes the ball, she gives me a big smile and a Thank you.

She knows how I like my sets when I'm tired, and she knows what to say to me when I don't feel like drilling.

Sometimes she gives me a look, and I just know that she wants me to cover more court.

All this, and we're both in bikinis.

Andy asks, "What kind of movies do you like?"

"I don't know," I say. I don't tell him that I haven't had enough money to see a movie since I moved to L.A. I say, "You pick the movie. But no violence."

We go to *Howard's End*, which Andy tells me is released only in L.A. right now, so I feel like a Hollywood insider.

We hold hands in the movie until they get sweaty. Then we let go, and then we hold on again.

At the end, the woman gets slapped at least three times. I cover my eyes, but I'm already shaking. Then I'm crying and I have a headache and I tell him we have to leave.

I feel like a moron.

In the car he says, "Are you okay?"

"Yeah," I say, "I told you no violence."

"I didn't know anyone got hurt," he says. "There were no warnings in what I read."

"Don't worry," I say, "I'll be fine." I hear the crack of the slaps the whole way home. When we pull up to my apartment, my face is wet and my nose is drippy.

He says, "I feel bad leaving you like this. Do you want to talk?"

"I come from one of those violent families," I say, and then I'm hysterical and I don't want to leave him like that, but I don't want to go into the family stuff, so I invite him up.

The closer he holds me, the fewer tears I have.

I say, "I'm not like this. Really."

"Don't be sorry," he says. "It's so nice to be with someone who has this much emotion. I envy you." I look at his eyes, to see if he's kidding, and he puts his hands on my face and kisses me. I put my arms around him and kiss back, and we make out on my carpet until the rug burns bleed.

ESTHER GETS A LETTER back from some professional autograph collector in Hawaii who says the signature on the cover of his 1955 *Life* magazine is a forgery, and he wants whoever signed it to pay. His estimate of the cover's worth, before it was defiled, is $10,000.

Heidi and I panic. Heidi gives the note to Esther and Esther says he's crazy and sends him four Esther Williams-brand swimsuits.

Esther tells me, "From now on, make the E's loopier."

SOME PHOTOGRAPHER is taking my picture while I'm serving. Laura says, "You should get paid for that picture. Everyone else does."

I usually turn down jobs that interfere with volleyball, but this commercial stuff seems like it's part of being a volleyball player.

Laura gets me signed with her agency, and two days later I get a call for a Bud Light commercial.

The commercial is being shot at Long Beach, which used to be a disgusting beach, but now there are volleyball nets and plastic palm trees. There are colorful beach umbrellas with beach scenes underneath, including picnic baskets, Frisbees, towels and Bud Light. The only thing missing is people.

The people are sitting in the parking lot playing Game Boys and reading the Hollywood Reporter. You can tell the difference between the volleyball players and the actors because the actors have yellow tans. The only difference between me and everyone else is that I'm reading Kafka, but I keep rereading the same page.

The director, or production assistant, or whoever she is, tells us to line up in our bathing suits. I'm wearing black, and she says, "Black. No one shoots a beach scene in black. What else do you have?"

"Nothing," I say.

She pulls out the volleyball players and sends us off to the nets. Then she divides the utterly beautiful from the ordinarily beautiful, and she motions the latter to stay in the background.

We have to play volleyball with a plastic orange ball that no real player would touch. The net is lower than a woman's net to make us look like superhuman hitters. Someone yells, "Action....cut," about six times an hour. I thought it would be fun to play volleyball all day, but they don't want volleyball, they want constant excitement, so we have to just throw the ball in the air and laugh and touch each other like it's a party. Each time someone yells, Action, the men take a little more liberty until everyone is too close and too touching and the action-cut person reminds us about the volleyball. I make it my job to keep the ball in the air because I don't want anyone to touch me.

The lunch is catered. I see people stuffing extra food in their bags. I want to do that, too, but the people who are stuffing are the not-as-beautiful people, who are not sure when they'll get another job. I take only what I can eat, which isn't much.

After lunch, we trudge back to the beach, and I look for a piece of glass to step on. I rub the cut into the sand to build globs of grainy blood. "I'm injured," I say to the person in charge of the trees. He takes me to the catering tent, and says I should see the nurse and forget about the rest of the shoot—they'll pay me anyway.

ANDY'S COMING to pick me up in twenty minutes and the pizza hasn't had enough time to digest, and I'm panicking because I can't go over to his house with a full stomach. So I take three gulps of milk and I jump up and down and do six somersaults to mix everything up.

I get everything out minutes before he rings the doorbell, but I still have to take a shower, so I pretend I'm not there.

I NEED SOMEONE to drill with because Laura's at her mom's for the week. I call Heidi. I leave a message. I call twenty times in two days.

She calls back the third day. She can't drill with me because she's making a documentary and she's getting a band together.

I say, "Do you have video equipment? Do you play an instrument?"

"I'm learning, okay? I'll have all the video gear by the end of the day. I'm calling everyone I know, and if that doesn't work, I'm charging it. I've got my guitar out. I'm making new recordings. I've got a call out to this singer I knew a while back. I have to go food shopping. I have to call you later. I'm really busy."

She hangs up.

I call back. "Heidi, are you on drugs?"

"Fuck you," she says. She hangs up.

I do three hours of jump serves so that when I get home I'm too tired to shower, and too tired to think, and I fall asleep fast.

A HIGH SCHOOL in Appleton, Wisconsin, is asking celebrities to list their favorite book and tell why. On a piece of Esther's stationery, I write, *"Blood & Guts in High School,* by Kathy Acker because the narrator says a good way for a woman to separate from her parents is to get a man as a substitute."

ANDY AND I are reading on his sofa. This is the perfect date. He's not fucking up my mind so much that I can't concentrate, and he's not ignoring me so much that I have to kiss him.

I stand up after two hours. I have to meet Laura at the beach. I change in the bedroom, and I walk around his house in my bathing suit collecting my things. I glance at him to make sure he's admiring my body.

He's not. Maybe he would, but last night I found two *Penthouse* magazines under his bed. The dates were old, and he said he was lonely and scared of women. But I bet that no matter how understanding I was, which I wasn't, he'd still be embarrassed.

I put on shorts and a T-shirt, put a ball in my backpack and stop to kiss him good-bye as I wheel my bike out the door.

I feel important having somewhere that I need to be.

Andy asks what magazines I read.

"None," I say. "I don't like sitting with something in my lap for a long time and then throwing it out."

Andy and I start making out on his sofa, and I'm not sure if I want to be doing this because I don't want him to lie to me, but he puts his magazine on the floor, and pulls himself on top of me.

Then the phone rings and Andy answers it.

It's Heidi. I haven't heard from her in two weeks. She's crying. She's running out of drugs, and could I come over.

When I get to her apartment, she's vomiting. She says it's from an overdose. Her cats are eating it.

One cat is dead from starvation and Heidi wants to have a funeral. I dig a hole while Heidi throws up. Heidi wants us to pick flowers and read poetry and find a rock for a gravestone.

When I don't hear anything, I go back inside, and she's swallowing something. "Heidi, you're just going to get sicker."

"Don't fucking tell me what to do."

The cat is stiff and bony, and Heidi wants to sleep with it one more night before we bury it.

▽

ANDY AND I are sleeping in his bed, in our clothes. I want to love him, but I don't think he's smarter than Cameron, and I know he's not better looking. I want to take off my clothes and blow him away with my greatness as a bed partner, but last time I did that was with Robert and it made me sick.

Andy says he's usually impotent.

"At the beginning?" I say.

"No. Pretty often, actually."

I think, Oh my god, this is terrible. I say, "Oh, all men are impotent sometimes, and men think it's a big deal because they never talk about it among themselves. Women know it's not a big deal."

He says, "Really?"

"Yeah," I say, and I hug him and panic that I will not be a sex goddess if he can't get an erection.

I WANT TO STOP stealing but it seems like such a waste of talent. So on the way to the beach, I have Cameron drive his rental car to Ralphs, and I run in and steal concealer.

I go into the bathroom at the beach and put it on my bikini line to hide the redness from where I tweezed.

Women at this beach hate to play co-ed, so I have to ask a woman who is not as good as I am, and she plays with us because she thinks I'll be her partner.

I ask this guy to play who plays on the men's tour, but off season he's a leper because he writes quotations from the New Testament on his volleyballs. Today we play with Galatians I.5.

After a few points, I realize that Cameron is not good enough to play at this beach. He doesn't stand still on defense; he over-commits and then can't make the play.

I'VE SLEPT OVER at Andy's six times and I still haven't taken off my clothes. I know it's time to take off my clothes, but every night I sleep over I have red bumps, and I put on concealer, but I'm scared the concealer will come off on his sheets.

I GET LOTS OF LETTERS from people in Sweden because there was an Esther Williams movie festival on Swedish TV. Most people send me international reply coupons, but one person sends me an SASE with forty three-cent stamps from 1908 pasted on the front of the envelope. I sell it to a stamp collector for fifteen dollars and I buy Andy the new Nine Inch Nails CD because he said he likes that I'm full of surprises.

ANDY HAS TO MOVE OUT of his apartment, so he's sifting through his stuff. I ask him why he saves everything and he says, "It's too hard to figure out what I really need."

I've decided that we should live together. It would save me lots of money, and I would have to stop throwing up.

When we get into bed, Andy gets all amorous, and I know if I mention moving in together, he'll never get an erection. So we start touching and kissing, and all of a sudden, Andy has this huge erection.

I wet his penis with my tongue and then slip him inside me.

When the sex session is over, I give him two minutes, and then I say, "Andy, why don't we move into your new apartment together?"

I kiss him with firm, erect tongue to remind him how special I am.

He says, "What about all your books? They take up so much room."

I kiss his neck and put my tongue in his ear. "That was great sex," I whisper.

"Okay," he says. "Let's look for an apartment tomorrow."

I WANT TO MIX our money, and Andy says, No way.

He wants to mix our books, and I say, No way.

So he pays $1,000 for bookshelves that can be attached to the wall.

I decide to put Nice Jewish Girls in anthologies. I put Bible commentary in literary criticism. I put Wanderings in history and Yiddish stories in fiction, and soon there is no more Judaism section to worry about.

CAMERON: I heard from the post office that you moved.

Me: What did you send me?

Cameron: A million dollars. That you're not getting because you didn't bother to tell me you moved.

Me: I moved in with Andy.

Cameron: What? You've only known him two months.

Me: It's a lot cheaper to live with him.

Cameron: What about being a lesbian?

Me: There are so many men willing to support me while I play volleyball. Besides, I love Andy.

Cameron: He's supporting you?

Me: Mostly. I don't ask him for money. He just sort of comes up with it when we go out to dinner or something.

Cameron: I'll give you money.

Me: No. I feel better taking it from someone I'm sleeping with.

Cameron: Is that a proposition?

Me:

Cameron: I think you're being lame. Why don't you get a real job so you can sleep with women.

Me: Why don't you get a real wife so you can stop sleeping with women?

Cameron:

Me:

Cameron: Look. I'm sure Andy's a really nice guy.
Me: I'll tell you one thing, he'd never cheat on me.

LIVING WITH ANDY means living with his rock collection, which is filled with stones he can't remember why he ever liked. Living with Andy means letting him cover our walls with art that has the emotional impact of an IBM spec sheet. My collection of art is in the garage, including the collage of Barbie parts that Heidi made.

Living with Andy means not flushing the toilet unless it's number two. We didn't start out this way, but I take a shower after every time I tweeze or throw up, and in Los Angeles the value of water is tied to the value of gold.

Living with Andy is lonely. Tonight he started watching TV as soon as he came home. I want the TV thrown out. "We need to make more room for books," I tell him. He switches to MTV, which he says he needs to watch for his work. I know he needs to watch so he doesn't have to deal with me.

If I didn't have mood swings he'd ignore me completely.

When Beavis and Butthead come on, Andy goes to the kitchen. He hates that there's never any food in the house. "Where does it all go?" he asks.

"I'm an athlete," I tell him.

He almost never eats at home anymore because there's nothing there.

I go into the bedroom and touch myself because Andy never touches me.

I go into the bathroom and pee, and I flush because I don't want to be near him.

ONCE THE TOURNAMENT season starts, Laura finds a new partner. In fact, everyone finds a new partner. In fact, everyone finds a new partner every week, and I feel like I'm in prom hell where I need a date for the dance every weekend. I decide that I would be willing to take a not-as-good-as-I-can-get partner if she were willing to stay with me for the whole tournament season.

RIGHT NOW, Andy has his hand on my breast. We haven't had sex in three days. This is my limit. Robert never ignored me like this. I am a volleyball player. I have a perfect body. Andy and I cannot be close if he does not appreciate this.

He falls asleep, and his hand goes limp on my breast. I move around a little to make it like he's running his fingers across my nipple, but this is taking more energy than it's worth. I get out of bed and answer Esther letters.

Bessie O'Madigan says her husband thinks Esther is the most beautiful woman in the world, and Bessie O'Madigan would like to give a photo of Esther to her husband for their anniversary.

I send a headshot from when Esther was sixty years old.

I NEED TO HAVE SEX. I want to crawl into our bed, into Andy's arms. I wish we could be having sex all the time, because then he would be attached to me.

He's at work now. He has no idea what I do during the day. Neither do I, so I don't like to start doing it until after he leaves. I'm always scared I won't do anything—won't play volleyball—and he'll find out. Then he'll dump me because the only thing I've accomplished in my life is to fill my emptiness with his penis.

I try to spend my day the way people who take care of themselves do. I sit at the breakfast table looking at Andy's empty chair and my empty cereal bowl and wonder what exactly those people do. What if I never do anything satisfying in my whole life? The thought is too scary so I have some bananas and peanut butter and some chocolate milk to wash it down, and when I finish I say to myself, OK, what should I do now? Then I go into the kitchen and make another batch of coated bananas. Soon even those three seconds when I ask myself, What now? are too much, so I bring the peanut butter, bananas and chocolate milk into the breakfast room.

Then I throw up.

I spend the rest of the day distracting myself from food. I masturbate. I make face masks. I wait for Andy to come home from work and carry me off to bed.

Then I'll be free from the temptation of food and I'll be able to do something productive with myself.

When Andy comes home, he holds me, he comes, he goes to sleep, and then he's as good as an empty chocolate milk container.

I STAY at my parents' house when the tour stops in Chicago. Since I can supply free lodging, I get a partner who can both hit and play defense: Christie. Very talkative. She asks my brother Marc what he does.

Marc says, "I'm getting a PhD in economics at the University of Chicago."

Christie says that would be good for working at McDonald's.

Marc says he wouldn't do that because their headquarters is in Arkansas.

Christie says they have stores all over the country. Christie calls

Illinois the East Coast. She calls the expressway from O'Hare the freeway.

"There's a toll," Marc says.

I say, "It's called a freeway in California."

I want to tell my family that Christie is a genius at knowing where to place the ball on the court. But my family is already excusing themselves from the table. On the way out, my mom says to me, "Sweetie, your brain is atrophying."

Christie asks what's wrong.

"My mom thinks playing volleyball is worthless and I should get a graduate degree."

"Doesn't she know you're making money?"

"Christie, we're only making enough to fly ourselves to the next tournament."

I wish Christie were a lesbian so I could chalk up this evening to a learning experience.

I read *The Federalist Papers* on the train to the tournament in case I decide to go to graduate school.

Christie is worrying that my brain will be too crowded with thoughts to concentrate on the game. I don't tell her that my brain is always too crowded with thoughts to concentrate on the game, and if my brain weren't always too crowded, then I'd be too good a player to be playing with her. "Watch for Addison," I tell her, "there's a great view of Wrigley Field from that stop."

I'm the only player from the Chicago area, so everyone watches me and Christie. Women I knew from high school tell me I have a great body. Men I knew from high school give me their phone numbers. Cameron trails behind me with an incredulous smile. For the first time, I am not worrying that he'll walk away from me in a crowd. For the first time, I don't care if he does.

In between my games, I leave Cameron in the bleachers watching Lucy Hahn—who is the only Asian woman on the tour—and go call Andy, who is not home.

"ANDY," I say, "I don't think we communicate very well."

Andy says, "I'll work on it."

I say, "If you could touch me more, it would help."

He says, "Okay."

We get into bed. I crawl on top of him, and catch his erection between my legs.

I expect him to touch me everywhere—to roll me over, and roll over me, and roll his head across my stomach and between my breasts. Instead, he rolls his hips upward and slips himself inside me.

I don't think he knows this is too soon, but I don't want to tell him because I want him to feel like we love each other.

I want to fall asleep hugging Andy, but I can't sleep with my arm around him because my shoulder is strained from volleyball, and when I'm not playing I have to keep it straight against my side.

MY DAD calls to tell me I'm on the cover of the *Chicago SunTimes*. I am excited. This will be great for getting more sponsors. I imagine myself looking powerful, crushing the ball, in color, with a caption that says how accomplished I am.

I call Cameron, and Cameron goes out to buy a copy of the paper.

He calls me back to tell me the photo is of my butt when I'm bent over. He says, "Only an old boyfriend would recognize it as you."

ANDY WANTS more friction. This morning he said he can't feel anything when I give him a blow job. Heidi says he's lying. "Does he come?" she asks. "People don't come without feeling something." But even though he comes, I'm still dreading getting into bed with him. "Do you use your hand?" she asks. "You have to use your hand."

I look at her.

"Look," she says, "as far as I'm concerned, blow jobs are messy. You have to get everything wet. Lick your hand a lot, that keeps the whole thing going smoothly. He's not going to stop loving you just because he thinks he could give a better blow job than you can."

She drives me to the jazz bar where I'm meeting Andy.

She stays because she thinks I'm a wreck.

"Andy's always late for you," she says. "why don't you hit on someone while you're waiting? Get in some practice blow jobs."

"I feel too fat to have sex tonight," I say. "I ate cookies all morning. How can he like it when I'm this fat?"

"You eat less than anyone I know. Good sex requires good stamina. Why don't you eat some carbohydrate nachos while we wait?"

"I'm serious. Heidi, don't you ever feel too fat to get undressed?"

"No, I don't, because no man I've ever been with has felt that way in his whole life, so why should I? Would you eat something for god's sake?"

"I just want you to admit that men get more excited about fucking a woman with a perfect body."

"Two minutes ago you thought the key to good sex was a good blow job. Look, I really have to go. Tell Andy I say hi."

I wish Heidi would stay all night. I still haven't done all the whining I want. I reach over the bar and swipe a lime out of the garnishing dish. Then I take some orange slices and olives, and soon I'm wolfing stuff down.

Andy catches me as he approaches the bar. "Cherry?" I say,

mouth full of maraschinos. He kisses me hello and gets maraschino all over his tongue.

"Couldn't you find any food at home?" he asks.

"I'm having a bad food day," I tell him. "I haven't eaten all day and I feel really fat and I know I'm not fat I just can't help feeling that way and I feel like you won't love me if I'm fat and I feel like you won't love me if I'm moody and I feel like you won't love me if I have a zillion problems and I hate that you're always late for me. It's not showing me any respect."

"I'm really sorry I was late," Andy says. "I know it bugs you. It's something I'm working on. I'm sorry you're having such a bad day."

Andy puts his arm around me and pulls my torso closer to his bar stool. I want to be mad at him and hate him, but it's too hard now because I like the hug.

The band comes on. I hate them, and it feels good to have an object for my hate. Andy asks if I hate them.

I nod.

We ride home in his car. I tell him I hate his car: a testosterone car with a German name that he pronounces with Nazi diction. He suggests that I might be being racist against Germans. I tell him I'm not racist against Germans; I'm racist against men.

Andy is quiet the rest of the drive.

By the time we get home, two men have complimented his car, and one man has complimented his chick.

In our apartment, I put on an oversized T-shirt and an extra large sweatshirt and melt into the sofa to sulk. Andy watches me. He sits down next to me.

"Don't touch me," I tell him. "I don't feel like being touched." Andy puts his hands in his lap.

"I just want to understand how you feel," he says, "I don't under-stand how food can ruin your day."

I think about trying to explain to him the importance of the food variable in the female mood equation, but I'm not sure, so I say, "I'm too fat to be with you tonight."

He says, "You look the same as you did last night."

"Well I don't feel the same," I say, "I feel fat."

Andy says all the obvious things, like my weight doesn't matter, and I look beautiful, and I shouldn't be so hard on myself. But it's not what he says, it's how he says it. He's trying hard to deal with me. He's being so valiant.

I kiss him to spare myself his kindness. I hate that Andy never has bad food days. I wish I weren't such an emotional weight for him. I know this is going to be the reason he dumps me.

I decide to give him a blow job so he forgets that my mood is ruining the night.

We make our way to the bedroom. I roll around with his body for a while, contemplating the intricacies of friction.

We roll around a long time, because I figure the closer he gets to ejaculation while we're frolicking, the less the ejaculation will depend on my technique. Andy's hand slips under my shirt, but before he can touch my fat I slide down his body where I'll be out of reach. I push him back down on the bed. In my mind, I play the role of dominatrix so I'll look too purposeful for him to think of undressing me. I give his side a swat so he lifts his hips for me to pull down his pants. His penis is hard and unruly, so it's difficult to keep it flat enough to get his underwear off. I pull his socks off, frantical-ly building up saliva in my mouth.

I lick my hand like a dog, leaving a spit globule right in the mid-dle. I've seen Andy masturbate, so I try to move my hand the way he moved his. I try to be really into this blow job—moaning and groan-

ing, making his penis the center of my existence—I've read enough
books to I know that if I'm excited then the blow job will be more
exciting.

Andy is growling. He only growls when things are going well. I
remind myself to thank Heidi tomorrow. I alternate my mouth with
my hand, and pray that he likes what I'm doing. Things are very wet,
and his penis is moving nicely through my body parts. Just as I'm
getting used to the mouth-hand thing, Andy comes—way in the
back of my throat, so I feel like I'm drowning in rubbing alcohol.

He pulls me toward him, and I feel thin and beautiful and I want
him to touch me everywhere now. But Andy has fallen asleep.

I GET BACK from my morning workout, and his plane has left.
I cry. He's been gone two hours. Already I'm scared. I knew I'd be
scared.

Maybe it will be good to remember the feeling of being alone.
I'm always running around telling everyone how important it is for
people to be alone for a while, which is weird because the only
thing I learned while living alone was that I hate myself.

I walk around the house looking for signs of Andy: A can of nuts
in the bedroom, the box from his computer in the living room, the
smell of his sweat in the dirty laundry. I cry some more. Then I go
to the bathroom and notice that Andy left the seat up. I sit on the
porcelain a while to think.

I decide to masturbate. Once I start in with the excessive mas-
turbation, it's hard to stop because it feels good, and it doesn't make
me fat.

When I've worn out all of my masturbating possibilities it's not
even 2 p.m. I tell myself how wonderful it will be to have the whole

house to myself. I put on The Cars, which Andy won't listen to, and I start scrubbing the floors and dusting underneath the bookshelves. When Andy's around, there's never a clear path through the hallway. Now I can make the path I've been wanting. I take two boxes that Andy hasn't unpacked since we moved in, and I put them in the storage area. I move some of my overcrowded books into the cleared-out area.

After three hours of cleaning, I sit down on the sofa and wonder what I'll do next.

HEIDI: I'm doing a reading tonight. I'm picking you up at five, okay?

Me: No. I can't. I haven't left the house in four days. I'm never leaving.

Heidi: And what is that achieving?

Me: I don't feel like talking.

Heidi: Fuck you. I'm so sick of you disappearing. You are such a shitty friend. Why don't you fucking share some of your feelings instead of running away? And fuck you for not coming to my reading. It's really important to me.

Me: I'm suicidal.

Heidi: How do you know?

Me: I can't stop looking for stuff to do it with. I can't stop planning my funeral.

Heidi: Tell Andy. Tell him about the vomiting.

Me: No. He'll leave.

Heidi: Then you have to come stay with me. You're a mess.

Me: No. I'm unplugging my phone. Good-bye.

I BINGE AGAIN. I eat Doritos and whipped cream because that's all we have left. I can't make it come up. I need bread to solidify everything, but if I go buy it, my stomach will have time to digest the whipped cream. My finger is not making things come up, so I start scratching the back of my throat. I taste blood and I feel slips of skin under my fingernails. I keep scraping until I feel like I have strep.

I bend a coat hanger to go way down my throat. I feel like I'm gagging, and I like it. I think I could kill myself this way if I push a little further. I think I could kill myself better if I took sleeping pills; I take five.

I put on Nine Inch Nails and dance around the house, waiting to trip and rip through my throat. On a one-foot spin, I have a sort of convulsion, and the Doritos and whipped cream fly all over the living room. All over my books. The whipped cream is red. I can't believe I'm not dead.

I look through the specks of vomit for the sleeping pills. I'm ashamed that I've made this mess and I can't even kill myself. I wipe the vomit off the books and onto my body. I push the vomit on the floor into a pile and lay my face in it.

When Andy opens the door, I wake up, but I don't lift my head off the floor.

He's quiet for so long that I have to look up to make sure he's still there.

"Is this vomit?" he asks.

"Yes. This is what I do when you're not home."

He says, "I think you're bleeding."

"Do you hate me?"

"What are you doing?"

"Hating myself. I hate myself."

Andy gets a warm washcloth and wipes my face. Then he kisses me, softly on the cheek. There's dried vomit everywhere—in my hair, in my hands. I can't believe he's kissing me.

ANDY ASKS ME if I could please come out from under the blanket to talk.

"No," I say, "I can't. You can talk to me while I'm under here." I curl up in a tighter ball on the floor.

"Well," he says, "how was your day?"

"You mean did I throw up? I hate when you ask me. I don't want to have to report to you every time I blow it. I'm trying, okay?"

"Okay." Andy sits down on the floor. He sits on the edge of my blanket and I have to tug it out from under him. He says, "I'm going to make myself dinner."

"Okay. Wait. No. Will you stay with me?"

Andy sits down in the chair next to me with *Mix Magazine*, and even from under the blanket, I smell his jelly sandwich.

IN CLEVELAND I PLAY with Tammy, who isn't great at serving, but she is great at talking on the phone, so she has more sponsors than anyone else on the tour. One of the sponsors is Delta, so we both fly for free. The hotel is free too, because Cameron meets us in Cleveland, and he pays.

Cameron spends the weekend saying things like, "She can't hit to save her life, but I'd do her anyway." I spend the weekend thinking about everything but volleyball, and telling Cameron I'm concentrating too hard on volleyball to pay attention to him.

Tammy throws a tantrum second round when the ref calls her foot fault. Everyone looks at her, which gives lots of exposure to all the logos on her bathing suit.

I smooth out the sand on my side of the court.

ANDY AND I ARE IN BED, and he is about to go to sleep without even kissing me. I can tell. I want to kiss him so passionately and emotionally that we cry. But he'd stop me in the middle and tell me he's too tired. So I say, "Andy, I've been stealing and I just want you to know so I don't feel like I'm hiding it from you."

He turns over to face me. "What?"

"Not much."

"How much?"

"Probably about ten or fifteen thousand dollars."

"What? Not much? That's a lot."

"Well, I mean, not much compared to the professionals."

"That sounds pretty professional to me."

"No. I mean, bank robbers and stuff."

"You're comparing yourself to bank robbers? Do you hear yourself?"

"Yes. I feel bad. That's why I'm telling you. I feel like my life has been filled with lies, and I'm trying to fix it, okay?"

"What's your plan. I mean, how will you stop doing this?"

"Well, I figured out that after I feel like I won't throw up anymore, I'll get a job. And based on how I feel after four days of not throwing up, I think I can start looking for a job in about a month. I figure that I won't be eating lots anymore, so I don't need to steal from the grocery store. So for this last month, I'll only steal from bookstores and Thrifty. And fifty dollars a week from Esther for my share of the rent."

"You're going to steal for another month?"

"Yeah. And that's all."

"No. No. This is not acceptable. I can't be in a relationship with someone so alienated."

"What? What are you talking about? I feel close to you. That's why I'm telling you."

"No. You feel no connection to anyone. How else could you steal from so many people? How can you do this? I just don't see how you can do this. What were you thinking?"

"I wasn't thinking. I just did it. It's like throwing up. I just don't think once I start."

"What else do you do like that?"

"What?"

He's quiet for a while. I want to think he's thinking, but his eyes are glassy. He says, "If it's like throwing up, then you can stop right now."

"I won't be able to pay my part of the rent."

"I don't care. I'd rather you not pay rent than you steal money for rent."

"I won't be able to buy anything. How will I get books?"

"Get a job. Esther is not cutting it if you're stealing like this."

"I would never make enough money. I would never spend the money right. I'd buy books. I'd get fired. Look how long that Crate &Barrel job lasted."

"Oh my god. Did you get fired for stealing?"

"Yeah."

He looks down. He's upset. I feel sorry for him.

He says, "You're an adult. You have to take care of yourself."

"Fuck you," I say. "I am taking care of myself. I'm not throwing up. Do you know how hard that is? You could never fucking know how hard this is. You are always so stable. Do you ever even fucking cry? I've been crying for four days. I am taking care of myself."

Andy holds me. "I'm sorry," he says. He clasps his hands together around my body, like he doesn't know if he should be holding me or himself. He says, "I'll pay rent this month. I'll buy food. You just concentrate on not throwing up. I know this is all you can do right now."

I say, "Thank you." Then I say, "If I get a job, I can't play volleyball."

"You can work at night," he says.

"But that's when I lift weights."

"Do you want to take care of volleyball or take care of yourself?"

"I don't know. I need to think about this, okay?"

"Promise me you won't steal anymore."

"I won't be able to pay rent."

"Promise me."

"Okay. I promise."

Andy turns out the light and rolls onto his side. I can't see his face, but from his breathing I can tell he's crying.

I READ FOR A WEEK. I read Cisneros, Coover, Camponegro, Carver and Cortazar, and that's the last of the Waldenbooks. I cry when I finish *Hopscotch* because I don't know how I'll get more books. I know it's stupid to cry over this. I know I could go to the library, but I have to own a book if I read it. I've given back Cameron. I've given back Robert. I cannot give back my books.

THE BOOKSTORE is dark and dirty. The shelves look more used than the books, and the man at the desk looks more used than the shelves.

"How are these organized?" I ask.

"They aren't," he says. "What are you looking for?"

I say, "I'm not sure, so I guess this is a good place for me because I can find everything wherever I look."

"Or you can find nothing," he says.

I smile, and turn around and start walking through the aisles.

The only place that's organized is the aisle in the back of the store: World War II. There is a fiction section, an art section and a section for every country that fought. I decide I'll read war novels. I pick out Hemingway, Vonnegut, Remarque and Trumbo and I sit down in the chair by the cash desk to decide which one to buy.

"You like World War II?" he asks.

"Yeah. Because it's organized."

"I was there. France. Best years of my life."

"Didn't lots of people die?"

"Yeah, but mostly Nazis."

His name is Gene and he wants to tell me war stories. He tells me about French prostitutes. Then I say I have to go.

He says I can have the books.

HEIDI DROPS OFF a load of mail. Usually Esther opens a few letters, just to see. In this batch, they're all opened.

"Why are they all open?"

"I guess she just felt like checking them all," Heidi says. "You know she's a control freak."

I thumb through the letters and notice the usual dollar bills enclosed for postage are missing. I usually swipe about 10 one-dollar bills an hour. I know there's no way Esther would take the time to fish out this money.

Heidi's eyes are red and her hands are shaking. I want to say, I can't believe you're taking the money I would be taking, but that's not true, because I can believe it. I say, "I'm not doing this anymore," and I give her back the letters.

I TELL ANDY I want to get married. I can't relax until I know he won't leave. I tell him I don't believe in people having casual living situations.

He says, "We need to know each other better. It's only been five months. I don't feel like I know who you are."

I don't know who I am, either. I tell him he's just scared. I tell him he knows me really well.

He says he'll think about it.

While he's thinking about it, I feel like I'm auditioning.

I tell him I can't stand this waiting, and he has a week to decide: Get married or break up. I know he'll choose getting married because he's too scared of women to find another.

AFTER THREE GAMES, I ride my bike to the bookstore. Gene lets me put my bike in the back because I don't have a lock.

He says, "I was hoping you'd come by."

"Yeah?" I say. "That's so nice. Why?"

"I need a Coke and I didn't want to close the store. Here," he says as he hands me some money, "buy yourself something, too."

I sit down in the chair by the desk.

Gene says, "You're getting sand all over the store."

"Oh. Sorry. I'll brush off outside."

"No, I was just wondering if people say anything about you wearing just that bikini top all over the place."

"No," I say, "only you."

"Well, in my day, that would be pornographic."

"It's only pornography if that's how your mind works."

"What?"

"If you objectify me, then our being together is pornographic."

"Well, I guess I'm objectifying you then. Is that bad?"

I hand him a copy of *Pornography and Silence* that is lying on the floor.

He gives me *Life in Pictures: World War II*, and we go through three more Cokes before I go home.

ANDY WANTS TO BREAK UP. I don't want to cry in front of him, so I go to the bathroom. I tell myself he's a liar for being in this relationship if he was thinking of breaking up.

I come out of the bathroom and say, "I'm leaving right now. I don't want it to be like Robert where we keep fucking until we want to kill each other."

"Wait," he says. "Don't leave now. I mean, you can stay for a while."

"Do you want to break up or not?"

"I don't want to get married."

"Why not? Why can't you ever make a decision?"

He says, "You scare me. You don't feel anything. You're so hard. There's no way you can love me."

"Fuck you. Then why don't you just dump me?"

"Because I love you. Or, I think I could love you. Well, I'm not sure. But I know I don't feel loved."

"Well I don't either," I say.

Andy says, "I think we should work together. Work on the relationship. I don't think it's time to get married."

I say, "Okay."

"I want you to see a therapist," he says. "I think you're too secretive to open yourself up enough to love someone."

"I want you to see a therapist, too. You never touch me."

"Okay."

We hug each other, and I hope he knows that he's paying for the therapy.

"GENE," I SAY, "Are you going to keep closing the store when you get tired? Why don't you hire someone to work here?"

"Because I can't find anyone. I want someone to run the whole store, I'm too old to haggle."

"I could run your store."

"You want that?"

"Yes."

"You have to understand the store, though. It has to mean something to you."

I think about what he's saying.

He says, "These books have been stepped on and torn, but they're beautiful—inside. Do you understand that?"

"Yes," I say, "I do."

I KNOCK on their bedroom door. "You guys," I say, "I have a surprise." There's no answer, so I walk in. "Breakfast in bed," I say, holding the tray. And then I say, "Ouch."

I get a splinter on Mom and Dad's wooden floor. I put the tray of hot chocolate and honey toast on Mom's side of the bed. Then I sit on Dad's side while he gets out a needle.

I hold my foot as still as I can in his hand while his other one digs under my skin to the splinter.

I can't see it, but it hurts. Dad digs deeper and there's a lot of blood. He sops it up with cotton. I hold still because if I make it hard for him he won't get the splinter out next time.

Afterwards, I walk around with a hop and a lean, and my dad says not to make such a big deal of the sliver, or I'll hurt something else much worse.

AT THE COCKTAIL PARTY, where I know no one and Andy knows everyone, I take a break and go to the bathroom. I lock myself in and relish sitting there on the toilet, in silence: No struggle to be entertaining, or to find Andy to rescue me from the social misdemeanor of standing alone.

After I pee, there's no other business I have on the toilet, but I sit there anyway, dreading my reappearance at the party. I figure I can stay in the bathroom for five more minutes without causing social discomfort.

I sniff my underwear. There's a strong smell from a long kiss during a slow dance. I sniff again, and I wonder why Andy doesn't take my used underwear to work with him in the morning.

The more I sniff, the more I want to go down on a woman. The more I sniff, the more I can't believe Andy doesn't go down on me every chance he gets. To punish him for not appreciating my scent, I think about the hostess while I masturbate on her toilet.

Then I go back out to the party and push my way into the circle where Andy is talking. He hates it when I get too dependent on him at parties, but I don't care now, because now I'm a lesbian.

While I'm standing silently at Andy's side, I play a game with myself. I play this game a lot because I can never decide if I'm a lesbian or not. I look around the room and imagine myself making love to various party dwellers, male and female. I always end up having better fantasies about the women. Their curves seem so soft to rub my cheek against. It always seems to me that my breasts would be more slithery across a woman's stomach than a man's.

"You have to mingle," Andy whispers in my ear. "Is something wrong?"

"Yeah," I say. "I think I'm a lesbian."

"Let's talk about it when we get home," he says. "For right now, why don't you just talk to the women?"

Andy is bored with my lesbianism. He figures since I've already tried women and stayed with men, he's doing fine. I want to say something like, Every time I scream when we're fucking, its because I'm pretending you're a woman. But that's not true, so I don't say it.

I THOUGHT MY LIFE was so ordinary that I wrote my sixth-grade autobiography about my cousin Jenny. In class we all hand bound our autobiographies, and I gave mine to my parents for their anniversary. My dad took it as a sure sign I would get into Yale. This Yale thing was a big deal to him, because we were the only Jewish family in the world who could become fourth generation Yale in this century. Dad figured that out. It was all up to me and my little brother, Marc.

Marc and I felt no pressure, though, because in our eyes every-one went to Yale. So at night, while our parents worked until 9:30, Marc and I would completely ignore our homework. We'd order-out pizza or Chinese food for dinner, and read the *Britannica* until someone came home to tell us to go to bed.

After a while, I noticed that the kids in school who had a lot to talk about all talked about TV. I told my parents I needed a TV. Mom told me to call up an electronics store and have them deliver one. This was the type of thing the spare Visa card in the kitchen drawer was good for. The TV came right away, but I never remem-bered to take it out of the box.

Once I called up my Mom at work and told her I didn't have any friends because everyone else's clothes were more exciting than mine. Mom told me to use the Visa card. She called ahead to a local store to let them know I had permission. "Next time, call Dad at work," she said, "not me." When I walked into the juniors section, I didn't see anything that I had seen other kids wearing, and even though I knew I could have whatever I wanted in the store, what I really wanted didn't seem to be there. So I bought a pair of rainbow socks that seemed nice in the store, but when I brought them home they didn't look special anymore, and I knew they would never win me friends.

Once a teacher asked me to stay after school. She was my favorite teacher ever, and I was hoping she would ask if I wanted to be her daughter. I had gotten stars on every test that year. Instead, she asked why I came to school bruised all the time. She said she thought maybe someone was doing something that ordinary parents don't do. I thought about the question for a few seconds, and then I looked down at my socks.

ANDY HAS BROUGHT the same copy of *Vibe* magazine on four business trips. When I investigate, I discover a very stained advertisement for Poco Jeans in which a woman is wearing nothing but jeans and earrings. Lots of earrings.

So I get my ears pierced. Seven times. I'd get my nipples pierced, but if there are infections and subsequent amputations, I'd rather lose an ear than a nipple.

The piercings hurt for a second. The piercing woman says they'll hurt more later.

They do. They have a dull, incessant hurt, and an excruciating hurt every time something brushes by them.

Andy takes the magazine to Montreal.

When he gets back, I don't even wait until we're out of the airport. I say, "It's painful to me that you fantasize about another woman."

"What?" he says.

"I noticed you brought that issue of *Vibe* with you for the nine hundredth time. Haven't you read all the articles yet?"

He blushes. He says, "Look, we've talked about this before. Its easier for me to masturbate with visual stimulation. I can't help it. That's just how I am. You use books, I use pictures."

"I feel like you're cheating on me. Like you don't need me in Montreal because you have her."

"I would like to have sex with you in Montreal, but you're not there. And this is not a person we're talking about, it's a picture."

"Yeah. That's right. That's why it's objectifying. Because you treat her like me, like a person, but she's not."

"Right. She would never put me on the spot like this in the middle of baggage claim."

I squeeze my ear really hard, until I start to cry. And when I let go I feel like nothing hurts at all.

MY PUBIC HAIR came late, and as soon as I had a nice covering, I cut it all off. I put it in a pile on a page of my diary, and covered it with a piece of paper, taped on all four sides. I wrote, "My PH's."

When the pubic hair grew back, it grew like eyebrow hair. So on nights when there was no eyebrow hair to pluck, I went lower.

I liked the quick, intense pain that rippled down my thigh with every hair I pulled.

Pubic-hair tweezing replaced eyebrow tweezing so my skirts could cover it up.

MOM WANTS to go shopping. She thinks if she buys enough dresses she can change her thirty-five-year-old body into a twenty-five-year-old body. She wants Dad to go with her.

I want to see *Grease*. I think if I see it enough times I can change my fifteen-year-old body into Olivia Newton-John's body. I want Dad to come with me.

Dad says he'll go to the movie now and go shopping at night.

Mom says I'm a spoiled brat and she's sick of scheduling her life around me.

I tell Mom she's a grouch and just because she's in a bad mood doesn't mean she has to take it out on us.

Dad gets nervous.

I say, "I'm sick of appeasing Mom when she gets in these moods."

Mom tries to hit me, but I'm big enough to slide to the side and then sock her in the stomach.

She yells at Dad. She goes to the refrigerator to get hard fruit for hurling.

At this age, I'm adept at dodging fruit, and it knocks over knick-knacks in the kitchen.

Mom's pissed. She hisses to Dad, "Stop her this second."

"Sweetie, please stop," my dad begs. "For me."

I want to protect Dad from Mom who walks over him, so I say, "No, tell *her* to stop."

His fist comes fast, too big to dodge. This is when I know to get up and start running.

I run in big circles through the library and living room, through the den and dining room, and Dad is not giving up. I'm slipping on wood floors and I'm screaming through doors and I don't want to fall because I don't want to stop, but I don't know where to run. Mom is screaming for me to stop screaming. She's in the kitchen trying to cut me off but as I run by I shove her into the stove.

I know this is stupid, running through my own house. I try to be rational, act my own age: "Dad," I yell out, "I'm too old to spank. Fifteen is too old."

"Then stop running," he yells as he slides through the hallway.

"You're going to get in trouble," I tell him.

"No," Mom yells to me from the kitchen, "you're the one in trouble."

I run through the breakfast room through the laundry room and I push over all the laundry to slow Dad down.

I run upstairs to rooms with doors, but he does two stairs for each of mine, and there's no time to shut doors behind me. He grabs me in the guest bedroom.

"Stop. You're hurting me!" I yell, before he is.

"Damn right I'm gonna hurt you," he says.

I wriggle away and scream, loud enough for Marc to hear on the third floor, but I know he won't do anything. Dad gets hold of my arm and it's taking too much energy for me to scream. The whole house is quiet. I kick him in the stomach and knock his glasses off. I have a plan to scratch his eyes out, but I'm always too scared. He gets hold of both my arms and knocks me down. "Dad, we're not doing this again. This is so dumb." He ignores me. He pins me on the floor face down and lies on top of me to hold me there. I stop arguing. I'm embarrassed and just waiting for it to be over—hoping he doesn't do anything that will show at school.

"Take down your pants," he tells me.

"I'm too old," I say into the carpet.

Dad has a totally rational tone to his voice now: "I'm going to let you get up, and if you run away, it's going be worse." He stands up and blocks the doorway.

I stand up and look at him. "I'm not doing this. You're going to be sorry. This is stupid. You don't have to do this."

"Just do it!" he yells, and the veins in his neck pop out. He's red and throbbing. He's sweating.

I take off my pants as he takes off his belt. He sits down on the bed and pulls me down with him. My face is in his lap and my arms dangle over his thighs. When he starts belting me, I bury my head in his lap so he doesn't hear me crying. Every time the belt hits, my arms wrap tightly around his thighs and he groans.

After a while, he stops. I am silent, sniffling-in as quietly as I can. I don't want Marc to hear. I don't want anyone to come in now.

I can tell there's no blood because Dad's hand runs so smoothly up and down my butt, in between my thighs. He is searching everywhere for blood. He won't keep going if he thinks I'm hurt.

When I think he's still searching, his hand smacks down. On my butt. On my thighs. He's aiming badly because he's hitting so hard. His whole body is moving with each swing, faster and faster and then, he stops. And rests his hand deep, in between my cheeks, and it feels good to cry, so I don't hold back anymore.

"All right," he says. "I'm done."

I can't move. I feel silly standing up in front of him without my clothes on, and anyway, my butt hurts too much to move.

Dad feels the wetness in his lap, and he picks up my face to wipe away the tears. And then he flips me over and puts my head softly against his chest. It moves up and down. His arms are around me, hands stroking me like a bunny. I am sniffling, taking deep breaths. He is breathing hard too. And I am so tired, I want to stay in this position forever.

He says, "Honey, I'm sorry this happens. I don't want us to fight anymore."

I hug him and apologize. I don't want to fight anymore either.

I SPEND MY FIRST WEEK at the bookstore organizing. I put all the fiction together by author. It takes me three days. Then I start on other sections.

Gene comes in to collect the money, and a customer asks if we have any John Hawkes. "We only have one," I say.

Gene says, "How do you know what we have?"

"I organized them," I say, and I pull the book off the shelf for the customer.

"I don't like it organized," Gene says. "It looks fake. Life is a mess, and books are about life."

I tell him I can help people better if I know where books are.

He says people will buy more books if they have to look around.

He goes to the shelf. "Look here," he says, "Marquis de Sade next to Gloria Steinem. This is a great pair."

I don't tell him that he's in the S part of my women's studies section.

I spend the rest of the week strategically deorganizing fiction—I mess it up enough for Gene but not so much that I can't tell what's there.

THIS IS HOW I meet Allie: I'm sitting with a group of people who I don't know very well, and I'm nervous, and I say, "I think my lover masturbates about five times a week." I know when I say lover people think I'm weird. But when I say boyfriend I feel like I'm referring to the kind of relationships I had in sixth grade, or the kind of relationships in Edward Albee plays, and I want to make it clear that I'm not falling into those patterns; I'm making my own patterns to fall into.

I mumble it fast, because if it takes a long time to get out, I'm not sure I could actually say it, and when I do, Allie says, "Oh my god, my mother does that, too."

⬇

ALLIE IS A RECOVERING MODEL.

She used to make two thousand dollars an hour. Now she shops in thrift shops with me, and sometimes she has so little money that she steals a three-dollar shirt. This is part of her recovery. "Living like the ugly people," is what I call it.

But she can't live like an ugly person, even in the thrift shop: A man stands next to Allie, who is standing in front of a mirror in an atrocious fake mink and fake leather coat. The man is as atrocious as the coat, and ten sizes bigger.

"You don't need that coat, honey, you look great even without it." Allie and I look at each other.

"Yeah," I say, "she really is beautiful."

"A real looker," he says.

"Yeah. I could look at her all day. Look at that chin. Perfect. And those exotic eyes." Allie turns toward the mirror to hide her laughter.

"Mmmm-mm. Don't see 'em like her too often. I'd sure like to take her home with me."

"Yeah. Me too," I say. Allie grins. She turns up the collar to hide. "I'd like to take her home and rip those clothes off and stick my wet fingers deep inside her."

The man looks at me.

"Wow. I'd really like that," Allie says, smiling. "I'd like you to fuck me right here under the clothes rack."

I meet Allie at yoga. She says, "When I saw you come in the room, and our eyes met, and I looked at your face, all I could think of to say is, I love you. I love you, I really do."

I know this is serious. I know it isn't the casual, friend-type I love

▷

you. She says it like a boyfriend does. Like he's giving his heart to you—or at least lending it. I say, "Thank you."

On our way to post-yoga breakfast, I say, "Allie, how could you tell me you love me in front of all those people?"

MY SEVENTH BIRTHDAY was five days away when my parents asked me what I wanted. I told them I wanted a chair to put in front of the living room window so that when I looked outside I didn't have to stand up.

"What do you keep looking at out there?" Dad asked.

"Lots of things," I said, "just look."

Dad looked. "I don't see anything."

"Do you see the tree in front of the Bly's house? Not the tall one. The small one. The one that has the point on top?"

"Yes."

"Now look at the branch poking out on the side."

"What?"

"Do you see it? The branch on the side. It's on the side near the shutter on the house. The one with only a few leaves. See how it bends? Right there at the center, it bends?"

"What?"

"It bends."

The next day, my parents told me that I was going to visit a psychiatrist. They said I was going to visit this man because I didn't have any friends. I assumed they were introducing me to him so that we could be friends, so I told my parents I didn't mind not having any friends. They said, "It's not normal to spend three hours after school every day looking out the window onto a street."

The next day I tried not to look out the window, but I couldn't do it.

The psychiatrist had on a suit and sat behind a huge wooden desk like my dad's. He had a map of the world, which I recognized from the encyclopedia. I wanted to check it out, but I didn't want to seem rude, so I just snuck a glance. He asked me my name. I told him. He asked me how old I was. I told him. Then he didn't say anything.

He was sort of twirling his pencil, and taking some bites on it in between twirls. So I pulled at the threads on the hem of my skirt. I thought he was weird for keeping me in the room if he wasn't going to talk.

When the yellow started coming off his pencil, he sent me out to the waiting room, and talked to my parents in his office.

The next day, my parents bought me a chair for in front of the window.

WHEN I WAS TWELVE I had a walk-in closet, with blue carpet on the floor, and green paint on the ceiling and that's where I would go to kill myself. There were shelves near the ceiling where my sweaters were lined up according to material. Velvety dresses and silky skirts hung below the shelves on either side of the closet, and a window let light in between. I sat under the clothes and felt sheltered.

Sometimes I'd do it with pills. I kept a constant inventory of all the pills we had in the house. I weighed them on the bathroom scale, and then figured out what percentage of my body weight they would be if I swallowed them all. Sometimes I'd arrange them alphabetically, sometimes by color. Then I'd imagine myself swallowing them, one by one if it was alphabetically, or one gulp for each color, or altogether if it was a day I did it by weight.

Other days, I'd curl up in the closet with my collection of *Soldier of Fortune* magazines. I bought *Soldier of Fortune* so I could get a knowledge of the market. I read that women use pills and men use guns, and I spent a lot of time trying to figure out why no one used both, in case one misses. I had this one fantasy where I took all the pills, and then quick, before they could have effect, I shot myself in the head with an automatic rifle—probably getting off a few bullets before I couldn't move anymore.

I had a lot of different scenes, but they always ended up at the funeral parlor, and my whole family was there. I always left my family a letter to read at the service. In the letter I tell them that it's not their fault, and I love them. Then my parents do a little speech about how wonderful I was, and how much they loved me.

My dad stands up at a podium and tells everyone that even though he used to complain about me a lot, I was brilliant. The smartest person he knew. He looks my aunts and uncles straight in their teary eyes and tells them I got the best grades of all the cousins. He says I knew more state capitols than even my mom.

MY SNOW WHITE STORY:

I look at myself in the mirror at work. The stark contrast between my lifeless dark hair and my pallid skin is disgusting enough to make me call up Gene and tell him I feel sick.

On the way home, I eat six chocolate-dipped butter cookies so I can fixate on their evil fat content.

At home, I get an apple out of the refrigerator to wash down the evil taste of butter cookie. I lie on the bed to think about my feelings. I take a bite of apple. I realize that I don't want to know why

I'm depressed. I distract myself with my fingers, imagining a bunch of knights in shining armor who drag me back to a secret cabin in the forest. There's a bed for each of them, and none for me. So I move from bed to bed while they call me Whore and Slut, with moans and medieval accents. My trembling hand drops the apple. I fall asleep just as the tears come.

When Andy gets home, he kneels next to the bed and kisses me.

GENE IS WORKING for me for a couple of hours while Allie and I go shopping.

When we get back to the bookstore, Gene is very excited. He bought a Samuel Johnson first edition for fifteen dollars.

"Gene," I say, "I thought you told me not to buy a hardback without the dust jacket."

"This is an exception. This one still retains some value."

Gene prices the book at $200.

I wonder how I'll ever know all the exceptions. I wonder if I'd have passed up the Samuel Johnson book for lack of a dust jacket.

WE WENT TO OUR SHRINK today. He says we're the only couple he sees that holds hands throughout the whole session. He assures us that doesn't mean there's not still stuff to work on.

"Are you both happy with your sex life?" he asks. We both shrug and say, Yes.

He says he's asking because sex is a good gauge of intimacy between two people, and it would help if we could be more specific.

I explain that we've both had to make some compromises—Andy

has agreed to go down on me, but he won't tie me up. Now things are okay.

Andy tells about the night I played for him the CD single "You Suck" by the Yeastie Girls.

"It's an import," I interject proudly. The therapist gives me a nod, but it's a shut-up-and-wait-your-turn-to-talk nod.

Andy says that the song was mean.

I say that the lyrics are genius, and give an example:

You say you want things to be equal and you want things to be fair,
but you're afraid to get your teeth caught in my pubic hair.
If you're lying there expecting me to suck your dick,
you're gonna have to give me more than just a little lick.
You better learn how, because it's your turn now,
You suck!

The therapist thinks I'm interrupting again, so he tries not to laugh. "What bothers you most about oral sex?" he asks Andy.

"Well," Andy says, "I *want* to like it, but I need time." The therapist nods, because he's a man, and he says that he doesn't think any man likes the taste at first.

Then Andy and the therapist talk about how society gives vaginas a bad rap, and this is what men grow up thinking.

I interrupt: "If Andy thinks I'm disgusting, then I feel bad about myself."

"Is that Andy's problem or yours?" asks the therapist. This is what the therapist says ninety percent of the time. I can't believe we're still paying to hear this.

Andy says it's hurtful that I'm so impatient with him. He says he's trying his hardest.

I say he should try more often.

The therapist says that time is up. He says we should remember that we have a really good relationship, we're just going through a rough spot. He compares us to the couple that has to leave his office ten minutes apart so they don't kill each other outside.

MARC AND I hear Mom breaking stuff and crying. We go downstairs. It's the blue and white set of dishes—she's doing it shelf by shelf and she's covering the kitchen floor. "Stay out of the way," she tells us. We stand there and watch her.

She tells us that Dad is a terrible father and a terrible husband and the most selfish person in the world and she can't believe she married him and he's coming home late tonight. "Too late," she says.

After the dishes, she starts in with the stuff in the fridge. Some of the eggs don't break. I'm impressed with their shells.

She finishes, and announces that it's time for bed.

As I'm falling asleep, I hear Mom crying softly.

I wake up in the middle of the night. I hear Mom crying. I crawl out of bed and knock on her door. "Mom, are you okay?" I only hear more crying. "Mom?" I open the door. It takes me a second to figure out what's going on. "Oh, Dad's home," I say, a little embarrassed and a little grossed out. I shut the door.

ALLIE AND I go to the beach. When we walk by the volleyall courts, I can't look. Everyone is getting better and I am getting whiter. I am getting flabby. Not as flabby as Allie. She has no muscle. I wave across the beach to a couple of volleyball players. I'm sure they think Allie and I are having sex because that's the only reason for a player to be friends with someone who's flabby.

"Do you miss it?" she asks.

"Sometimes," I say, "but you can't have real friends on the circuit because everyone's always trying to dump their partner for someone better."

"I'll be your friend."

"My muscles are atrophying."

"So? Look at mine," Allie says.

"Yeah. I see that. How could you model with no muscles?"

"After a good shoot, muscles can be drawn in."

We put down our towels close to the water. All we brought are towels and sunscreen. It feels weird to be at the beach with no balls.

Allie says, "Why did you quit?"

I say, "Do you understand how good I was? I mean eight hours a day. Running in the sand, lifting weights. I was great. I can't relax until you realize how great I was."

"I think you're great now. I'm really glad to be at the beach with you."

"Okay, but I want you to be impressed with what a great athlete I am. I worked really hard at volleyball."

"I am impressed. You still look like an athlete."

"I do?"

"Yeah. Especially your legs."

"Okay. Good. Thanks."

We rub sunscreen on each others' backs and lie side by side, toes in the sand.

I TELL ALLIE I need new lipstick, and she tells me I have to buy Mac.

"Mac what?"

"It's a makeup brand. It's the best. It's the only kind models use. Good models."

"What about Estée Lauder? What about completely allergy-free, animal-testing-free, fragrance-free Clinique?" I display all my make-up knowledge in two sentences.

"No. Mac."

At this moment I realize that Allie really does know a lot about makeup; I know Crate&Barrel glassware and Allie knows makeup. So I bring her with me.

At the makeup counter, all the women look alike: exotic, mysterious faces, with lots of perfectly applied makeup. I feel out of place with my freckled skin and Barbra Streisand nose.

Allie becomes a new person. She is the professor. She is the TV commentator. She is the lecturing date. She knows the color names of the lipsticks better than the women who work there. Allie picks out a brownish color that I would have thought was only for brown people; it makes my face look mysterious. Then Allie puts a whitish color on the inner part of my lips, and tells me it's a trick to make my lips look fuller. They do, and now other women are watching Allie work.

When she finishes my lips, she starts on her own face using eye shadow for blush and lip pencil for eye liner, and the women who work there keep telling her she's doing it wrong, but then they become silent, because Allie looks stunning, as if she has on no makeup, and all the makeup in the world, at the same time.

IT TAKES SEVEN HOURS to drive from the airport to Sanibel and all we see is water.

On the beach, we are up to our knees in shells. The first day, we each fill two buckets I fill mine carefully because Dad says we can only fly home with the two hundred most perfect shells. Marc fills his bucket with clams. Mom says, "Why don't you get some snail shells or conchs? You can get clams on Lake Michigan."

Marc stops where he is and sits down on a pile of shells. He slowly dumps out all his clams. "I'll just use some of your shells," he tells Mom. He puts his empty bucket in his lap.

I give him some of my cracked conchs to make him feel better, and then I wander down the other end of the beach looking for perfect shells.

Dad follows behind me. While I'm crouching on the wet sand, Dad walks up to me with a big smile. He puts a shell up to my ear. "This is the ocean," he says. "Do you hear it?"

"How did you get the ocean?"

"It's magic. I'm giving it to you," he says. I hold on to the shell all day. I don't put it in my bucket because I don't want it to get mixed up.

We fill our buckets until the tide gets high. Then we go back home to the condo and we find lizards everywhere—in lampshades, in garbage cans. Hundreds. Mom screams, and when she screams, Marc and I scream. Dad screams, "Don't scream. You're scaring the kids."

"Well do something!" Mom yells.

Dad takes a broom and wooshes them off the walls and out the door.

When the lizards are gone, Mom cooks our dinner and Dad cooks our shells, to make sure the animals are dead. Marc and I stand by the stove to watch the animals float to the top of the boiling water.

After dinner, Marc and I can't move. Our skin feels like it will break. Dad says we are sunburnt. Mom says we are all sunburnt. We are so sunburnt we don't have to take showers. We are so sunburnt our clothes scrape our skin, so the next day we don't wear any.

We stay inside the whole day, and we all have headaches. Mom sits on the beach in a turtleneck and pants. Dad helps us to put Noxema all over ourselves because it feels so cold. We eat cold things for dinner. We go to bed cold on the outside and warm underneath.

Mom wakes us up in the middle of the night. She says it's low tide, and we can go shelling in the dark when the sun won't hurt. Dad carries Marc to the beach. I carry Marc's bucket. Mom lets Marc collect clams—he's too tired to find anything else. Mom brings extra buckets for us to fill because in the dark we might not see cracks in the shells , so we'll need to get extra. I have to dump out some shells to carry my buckets home.

The next day we wake up late. Dad cooks shells. Marc and I sort the good shells from the cracked shells and we put water on the good shells to make them shiny again. We put Noxema on each other to make us cool again. Mom comes back from the beach with pages and pages of writing that she won't read to us. They are letters to herself. She's not sending them.

Mom kisses me good night but she looks away and misses and gets just a little piece of my lip.

I turn over in bed to see what she was looking at. It's a lizard. I know she won't want me to know. I crawl into Marc's bed.

"Why are you in my bed?" he asks.

"I want to show you something," I say. And I reach under the bed to get my shell, and I say, "Listen. It's the waves. It's magic, and we have it right here, to ourselves."

ALLIE CALLS ME UP because she's rich. "I got a residual check," she says.

"What's that?"

"It's what you get every time a commercial runs on TV."

"But you haven't done a commercial in two years."

"A Bud Light commercial ran in Mexico three times."

"You were in a Bud Light commercial? So was I."

"I had a speaking part," Allie says.

Now Allie has money to buy gas, so we drive down Ranchero Boulevard in her red BMW which is not registered with the DMV because registration is expensive.

I pretend Allie is the red-BMW-rich model she used to be, and that makes me feel more beautiful.

Allie washes her car once a week.

I tell her that in Illinois, people don't wash their cars all winter.

"Oh, right," she says, "and I bet they don't take showers all winter, either."

"Allie," I say, "maybe you should model again so I could see what it's like."

Allie says, "After I got sober, I took a new head shot, and my agent wanted bare shoulders, and I wouldn't do it, and then the only auditions he could get me were for lesbian parts."

"You don't look like a lesbian. You have long nails. Lesbians can't have long nails."

"What?"

"Fingers in vaginas. Fingernails would cut."

We drive to The Ivy, where it's a hundred bucks a person. I wear a dress. Allie wears jeans and a T-shirt. Everyone at The Ivy wears jeans and a T-shirt. I realize that this is the uniform of people-in-the-know in L.A. I want to throw out all the clothes I bought that I thought would make me look like I'm from L.A.

"Allie," I say, "do I look like a geek?"

"You look beautiful," she tells me.

"I feel bad spending money that you had to prance around in a bikini to earn."

"What should we do? Throw it out?"

We order two extra meals to freeze for when Allie is poor again.

Then we go to the haircut place. We sit next to each other, and I get almost all my hair cut off. Allie tells the hairdresser to do whatever he wants to her. He cuts her hair straight across on the bottom, and when he finishes he tells her he gave her the haircut of her life and she looks like a model, and he'll give her free haircuts if she'll pass out his cards to people she knows.

My haircut is $75.

I FINALLY GOT INVITED to one of the seventh-grader boy-girl parties, but my Dad said we were celebrating Purim at his sister's house that night, and everyone in the family was going, and there would be other boy-girl parties. He told me when I grew up, I'd realize that in the long run, family holidays are more important than going out with friends, and for right now it was his job to make sure I prioritized correctly.

I RSVP'd that I would be going to the party just in case I could think of a way. On Tuesday, I baked hamantaschen for my dad, and at dinner I explained to Marc that we eat three-sided cookies because Haman, the bad guy of Purim, wore a three-sided hat. On Thursday, I went to synagogue with my father to celebrate Purim. That was a big favor. Usually, Dad went alone because the rest of us thought the Purim scene was humiliating. Everyone danced around the Torah, and I did that, too, to show my dad that I was dedicated to the celebration of Purim, just not that Friday night.

Friday, at school, I told everyone that I was going to the party, even though I hadn't really gotten permission—which made me nervous all day because so many kids were talking about the party that I knew I would be a total outcast if I didn't go; I'd miss everything. People might even *kiss* there, and I wouldn't know until Monday.

After school on Friday, I dawdled home, hoping that God would cancel Purim, or at least burn down my aunt's house. When I got home, both parents were back from work early. They never came home early. They were yelling.

I sat on the front steps and listened, hoping for some juicy information that I could use to get myself to the party. Mom was yelling about how holidays with my dad's family are absurd because my dad's family hates my mom. My dad was trying to convince her that this didn't matter. My dad said, "We're all Jewish, we can all celebrate together." My mom said she'd rather celebrate Purim with the PLO. They argued more, and finally, Mom said she wasn't going, and Dad stormed off.

This was my cue. I went inside, and asked my Mom if she'd drive me to the party that night. She looked down and she looked angry. "Mom," I said, as lovingly as possible, "its a boy-girl party, and it's really important to me." Finally, my mom said Yes, and it was the best Purim ever, because I was one of the people who kissed.

"BOOKSHOP."

"Hi, it's Gene."

"Hi."

"Oh," he says, "you need me to come in? . . . When? . . . That soon? . . . How about twenty minutes?"

"Gene, that was a great performance. Say hi to your wife for me."

"Okay. Well, I'll see you soon."

I read quickly to the end of *Sexing The Cherry*, because when Gene comes to visit I can never get any reading done.

ON THE FIRST NIGHT of Chanukah I give Andy two CDs. Andy already has 2,000 CDs, but I know I can pick anything he doesn't have and he'll like it—as long as it's not classical. I get him Bikini Kill. The lyrics are very women-oriented so Andy feels like a hip-feminist male just for owning a Bikini Kill CD. And I feel cool having a boyfriend who listens to it.

On the second night I give Andy bubble bath, because he likes sweet, romantic things. He's surprised because I'm never sweet and romantic. We light three Chanukah candles and bring the menorah into the bathroom, and slide into the raspberry-rhubarb bubble-bathed tub. I lie back against the tub and Andy lays his back against my chest. I wrap my arms around his waist, and his arms wrap around my thighs, and I nuzzle my nose into his soft blond hair.

On the third night I give Andy pruning shears.

"Thanks," he says, "these will make it so much easier for me."

"No," I say. "They're for me. I'm going to help you so I don't have to talk to your mom for an hour while you prune her bushes."

On the fourth night we have a fight. I return the shirt I bought him and buy a shirt for myself.

On the fifth night I give him boxer shorts covered with my finger-painted hand prints.

The sixth night I give Andy trees. Two hundred redwoods for his model train. He mapped out a replica of the Santa Cruz line at the turn of the century, and the model is almost finished except for the barren plaster that's supposed to be a mountainside. I suggested he put in bushes, which you can find at any hobby shop. He said, "You can't put *bushes* where *redwoods* go. The scenery isn't just there to cover up the foundation. Don't you get it? If I wanted to do *bushes*, I'd do a model of an *Illinois* train." So I scoured Southern California for a shop that sold redwoods.

On the seventh night I give Andy my other train store purchase. When I was wandering around the N-scale section, which is the inch-high train sets, I noticed a whole wall devoted to models of people—people who are less than one inch high, but covered with interesting details. The most interesting detail was that most of the one-inch people were men, doing things like reading a newspaper or playing tennis or buying and selling ice cream. The women were lying down in bikinis, or posing in tight shorts, or hanging out laundry—twelve different versions of women hanging out laundry.

"What are these for?" Andy asks, trying not to seem ungrateful for the gift.

"The model train. I thought you'd like some people."

"But where do they fit into the model?"

"Well, I think it's important to bring to people's attention how sexist the model train industry is."

"What?"

"There were no models of men doing housework or posing on the beach."

"I knew you wouldn't like going to train stores."

"You can put the women hanging out laundry in the forest, so they're like a colony of women whose lives consist of cleaning other people's clothes. What else could the manufacturer of these women have been thinking? Or they can be Stepford wives, and you can put them in your suburbs, on the front lawns."

"What about these other people?" he asks.

"You can put the sunbathers on the beach, and the other women on the boardwalk. And that guy who looks like he's buying something? That's the john for one of the women. Isn't that clever?"

"I get your point, but I don't really want to turn my model train into a monument to feminism."

"If you were really a feminist, everything you do would be a monument to feminism."

"How about if I give you the beach, and you can have the prostitution scene . . ."

"Sex worker."

"You can have the sex worker scene, and the beach bunny scene, and we can trade in the women washing clothes for people playing volleyball? The colony of Stepford wives seems a little over the top. Let's just leave the forest alone, okay?"

"Okay. Isn't it nice that we've found a hobby we can share?"

"Yeah, okay, but you're just sharing the beach, and that's all, all right?"

"Thank you."

"When is Chanukah over?"

On the eighth night I give Andy a blow job. It's not like this is something that I wouldn't do if it weren't Chanukah, but I want him to remember it's always a gift.

"DO YOU LIKE IT GOOEY or hard?" I ask Allie.

She says gooey, so I put her cheese sandwich next to mine in the toaster oven.

Andy is watering plants. He asks me to leave him some bread.
Allie asks him what he's doing today.

"Oh, I don't know," Andy says, "I guess I'll go to the office."

I look at Allie, and she raises her eyebrows.

I say, "Andy, do you want to come with us to the beach?"

"Yeah," he says, "if you two don't mind."

Allie says, "We'll make you a sandwich."

I make Andy a sandwich. Hard.

By the time we get down to the beach, the gooey cheese is hard.
Allie and I give our sandwiches to Andy, and we go to the popsicle
stand.

Allie orders a push-up and I get a rocket.

I tell Allie I hate women who can't go anywhere without their
boyfriends, but today doesn't count because she provoked me into
inviting Andy.

Allie says, "I don't mind having him along. I think of him as an
extension of you—when he's with us, he doesn't say enough interesting things to count as a third person."

"Oh," I say, and I don't know if this is good or bad, and I don't
have time to mull it over because the red is dripping onto the white
and the blue is dripping onto my hand, and Andy is waiting for us
back at the sand.

MARC AND I take a taxi to Hebrew school every Tuesday and
Thursday at 4:30. We're in different grades, but we both seem to
know the same amount; in fourth grade everyone learns the alpha-
bet and the sounds the letters make and the vowels—the vowels
don't count as letters because they sit on the bottom of the line like
sharks, and even though you never look that low, you can't forget

they're there. By fifth grade, everyone is smart enough to know that grades in Hebrew school don't count for anything—everyone passes if their parents pay synagogue dues—so fifth and sixth graders never do homework. And if you *do* do homework, everyone makes fun of you.

We used to be in a car pool, but Mom can't drive in the car pool because she works, and the other moms didn't want to send their kids in a taxi on Mom's shift. Salvador is the man who drives us.

The best day of Hebrew school was the day I convinced Marc to ditch with me. Marc didn't want to do it, but I told him if a teacher caught us, I'd say I forced him.

"What about Salvador?" Marc asked.

"Salvador doesn't care."

"What if he tells Mom?"

"I'll take the blame," I said.

We waited until Salvador pulled away from the synagogue, and we hid in the bushes so no teachers would see us.

When the coast was clear, I told Marc I had a surprise.

"What?" he asked.

"I brought money so we can go get ice cream."

"Oh my god. We're going to get caught. We're not doing that."

We ran a block to the ice cream store. Then we ran all the way back with our ice cream cones.

We sat in the dark cozy bushes, against the synagogue wall, eating our ice cream, reading Hebrew out loud to each other. And the only time I can remember loving the sound of the language was hearing it that day, in Marc's voice.

EVERYONE IN MY CLASS has seen *Saturday Night Fever* except me. I can't go because it's rated R, and neither of my parents want it used against them in divorce court. At first I think this is a bad situation, because I've earned the respect of my classmates by being the first to see *Shampoo*. But then I realize that my parents are fighting over who gets to have me, which is exciting.

I start keeping track of how my parents treat me so I can tell the judge the facts.

My parents buy me *The Boy's and Girl's Book About Divorce*.

I decide it's going to be a hard choice between parents, and I think a lot about the possibilities: A heated courtroom battle, where lawyers ask me lots of questions that my parents wish I didn't know the answers to, or I sit in the judge's chambers, and tell him all about my parents, and I start crying, and he holds me in his arms and tells me it's okay, and he'll make the final decision.

One day, I come home from school, and both parents are in the library—Mom in Dad's lap. I've never seen them sitting like this. It looks stupid. "What are you doing?" I ask. My dad says, this is a special time for them, and I should leave them alone.

The next morning, before school, they tell me they're not getting a divorce. "Why not?" I ask.

"We're going to Greece instead," Dad says, "all of us. Isn't that exciting?"

I LOVE CHRISTMAS because there's nothing to do. It's a day when Mom sleeps really late, and Dad gets up and makes pancakes with strawberry syrup for me and Marc. Then Dad makes a fire in the living room, and somehow Mom always manages to come down right when the house gets warm and cozy, and she turns on a radio station that plays Christmas carols.

Dad says he hates Christmas carols. Mom says we only hear them once a year, he can live with it. Dad tells us not to listen to the words. We spend the day reading in the living room, eating bologna sandwiches, not listening to the words.

Today, Marc and I decide to do homework because we're the only Jewish kids in school, so it's a sneaky day for doing homework because no one else can.

In the afternoon, Marc and I take a walk around the neighborhood to look at people's Christmas lights. We tell Dad we're going sledding.

It takes us twenty minutes to get on all our snow gear and find two pair of mittens, and then we have to scrounge the sled out of the basement.

It turns out that the snow is too soft and deep to pull each other on the sled — it keeps sinking, which makes it too heavy to move. So we take turns pulling the empty sled. There's lots of new snow, and we make the first tracks, which is what Jews get to do when all the Christians are opening presents.

Our whole neighborhood is lined with short brown lunch bags that have sand and a candle inside so that they work like lanterns. Each household is responsible for placing lanterns every three feet along their part of the sidewalk. My dad says that this is an astonishing example of communal cooperation, even if it is in the name of Jesus Christ. My parents won't participate themselves, but they give our next-door neighbor, Mrs. Bly, permission to put lanterns in front of our house so that we don't break the pattern with our Jewishness.

When Marc and I get back with our sled, Mrs. Bly is decorating our sidewalk. We all smile at each other, and she wishes us Happy Holidays which really means, Merry Christmas to those of you who don't celebrate it.

After dark, we look down the street, and it looks so orderly with the paper bags' glow resting orangely on the soft new snow.

A WOMAN COMES INTO the bookstore with black hair and black eyes and black clothes and black boots. She says she has Cher's check and would I accept it.

I say, "No."

She says she's Cher's personal assistant and everyone takes Cher's checks and I can call Cher if I want to.

I call Cher's bank, and I give the woman the phone. "Hi," she says, "This is Susan. Can you *please* tell this *clerk* to accept Cher's check?"

The bank is willing to claim Cher as an account holder.

Susan says Cher needs twenty-five feet of black books.

"Black?" I say, thinking Angela Davis.

"Black," she says, and points to a book about Greece with a black binding.

I round up twenty-five feet of black hardbacks with no dust jackets. I get some romances out of the alley where I also find six copies of Michener's *Jerusalem*. Susan finds a first edition in mint condition of *Diving Into The Wreck*. She puts it in her pile. I sneak it out of her pile and put it back in my pile behind the cash desk where I keep books I've priced too high for reasonable people to think of buying.

Susan pops a bubble in my face and writes a check for $2,500.

It's Gene's biggest sale ever, and I buy him a Sonny and Cher tape to celebrate.

I WANT TO KILL all the people who made me believe a boyfriend will save me.

MOM, MARC, ME AND DON MCLEAN are all singing, "Bye-bye Miss American Pie." Marc asks what she looks like, and Mom says, "Light brown crust and cherry filling and ice cream on top of her head."

"Yuuummmm," Marc says.

"Ssshhhussh," I say, "you're ruining the song."

We are driving to The Gingerbread House, which is the place we go while Mom's at work. The drive there is an hour long, so we know all the radio songs. Mom says that before we used to go to The Gingerbread House, before I can remember, we stayed at home with baby-sitters, but she says one baby-sitter hit us with a brush, and the other baby-sitter forgot to come some days. I want to try another baby-sitter, but Mom says No.

When we get to The Gingerbread House, we all get out of the car, and Marc starts to cry.

"Sweetie, tell me why you're crying," Mom says.

Marc says that yesterday he wet his pants, and the teacher yelled at him and told him he was a baby.

"Well," I say, "he is a baby, sort of. Four is almost a baby."

"That doesn't mean she had to yell at him," Mom says, squooshing Marc in between her arms.

"But Mom," I say, "the teachers yell at us all the time."

"I know," she says. "Okay, look, you two can come to work with me today."

Marc stops crying right away.

Mom works at Kemper Insurance Company and there's a huge golf course at her office where we have picnics. Mom is in charge of two hundred people, and Marc and I introduce ourselves to them all. They are mostly dads, but they don't bring their kids. Mom tells us not to bother anyone, but everyone says they don't mind. Mom has a punch card machine with five different colors of cards. Mom has a phone with buttons that light up, and we want to use it, but we have no one to call. "Can I call Dad?" I ask.

"No. He's too busy at work," she says. "Why don't you call Marc on the phone next door?"

Marc and I talk while Mom works, but we don't have much to say, so Mom doesn't work very much.

Mom takes us to lunch. We go to Jack-In-The-Box and we go with Charlie, because his office is next door, and I invite him.

At lunch, Charlie asks me if I want to be like my mom when I grow up. I say, "No. I want to be in charge of things, and Mom says that Kemper doesn't like to let girls be in charge."

Mom asks me if I need to go to the bathroom.

I say, "No."

We go anyway, and she says I should never talk about her job in front of other people.

After lunch, Mom brings us back to The Gingerbread House.

I'M READING KATHY ACKER and I'm getting really wet. That's what happens when I love a book. Andy asks what I'm reading. He probably smells that I like it. He's probably hoping I'll get so excited I'll put the book down and fuck him. It's happened before. That's the only shortcoming of books—they're asexual.

I show him the spine. "Why do you like reading her so much?" he asks.

"She always tells stories about weak women." He tells me I need strong female role models—that if I were really a feminist, I'd know what I want to do with my life.

I flip to the back cover and look at the author's photo. Andy thinks he knows everything. He says he hates men for being closed-minded about women.

I try to imagine being the strong, completely unneedy, financially huge woman that Andy wishes he could be with.

If I were that woman, I can tell you one thing, I wouldn't be living with Andy.

GENE COMES IN to chat. "Why are you reading? You're supposed to be working," he says.

"There's nothing to do," I say. "All the books are priced and shelved."

"There's always work. You can dust."

"Gene, don't make me laugh."

"You have no work ethic. You're a slinker."

"The term is slacker," I say. "Did you have a fight with your wife?"

"Not a fight. She just bothers me. I want to talk about death and the universe and she wants to talk about groceries."

"Gene, I bought this book for you." I pull out from my hiding place under the desk a book with pictures of how huge the universe is and how insignificant we are.

"How much did you pay for it?" he asks, which is ridiculous since we pay less than any used bookstore in L.A.

"Five percent of the cover price," I say.

Usually we pay ten to twenty percent, so I expect him to be happy, but he says, "Don't steal from the people who bring in books."

Gene sits down in the chair with the universe in his lap.

One of the regulars comes in. Each week he scavenges four terrible paperbacks that I throw out. I give him two dollars, which he uses to buy Burger King stuff across the street. He says hi to Gene. This scavenger has been selling books to Gene for ten years.

Gene mumbles, "She's in charge today," and turns the page.

A woman comes in with the same shitty romances the man sold us. I say, No thanks.

She says the books will sell.

I say I know, and I think that's sad, and I don't want to be a part of it.

She says she brought them all the way from the Valley, and I should just look through the box.

I look through the box, and underneath Judith Krantz and Joan Collins is a layer of diet books from the sixties.

"I'll give you a quarter each for these," I say, holding up the diet books.

"How about forty dollars for the whole box?" she says.

"No. We don't buy books by the pound."

"Then I'm throwing all the books out." She says, "I have never been so insulted in my life. Some of these paperbacks have never been opened. They're worth seven ninety-nine each."

"I'll give you ten dollars," I say.

"No." She snatches the books out of my hand and starts to leave with her box.

"Okay," I say, "forty dollars."

When she leaves, I throw the romances in the alley and put the diet books in my hiding place.

Gene says, "Are you crazy?"

"I wanted the diet books to save as evidence."

"*You're* paying for them yourself, right?"

"Okay, fine."

"Evidence for what?"

"Look, this one says eating three hundred calories a day is good for women. This is the systematic torture of women by the medical profession," I say, shaking the book at him.

Gene says, "That woman on the cover is very attractive."

ALLIE HAS $100 left over from her last residual check and she wants to take me to the Whiskey, which is a club where she used to hang out with another sixteen-year-old and Jack Nicholson and the owner in the back room. "Who's playing at the Whiskey?" I ask.

"That's not the point," she says. "I'm having a reunion with my past. I'm facing the place where my innocence was lost."

Allie would never be melodramic unless it were really important, so I bribe her: "I'll only go with you if you'll show me your portfolio."

"No. I told you no. I'm not even sure where it is anymore."

"You know where it is. You told me you rearrange it when you get depressed."

"My portfolio is depressing to look at it. You'll get depressed. I look like an idiot."

"Maybe you should get someone else to go to the Whiskey with you."

"Fuck you."

"I won't be able to put the Whiskey in context unless I know what you looked like when you were modeling."

"Remember that picture of Jack Nicholson in the *Enquirer*? I looked like that woman with him, but I was underage."

Allie keeps the portfolio under her bed. It looks like a normal photo album. I sit on the edge of her bed, and she puts the portfolio in my lap.

I hold it with both hands. "Okay. When is this from?"

"When I was eighteen to twenty-three," she says. "Are you going to open it?"

"Okay, okay." The first picture is of Allie in a Polo ad, and she's swimming in brown tweeds. Her lips are huge and red and her face looks airbrushed. Her hair is perfectly messed and her sweater is perfectly wrinkled. I look up at her to remind myself what she really looks like, but she's not as nice to look at as the picture. I want to take the picture home to study it.

"I was totally hung over when they took that picture," she says.

I want to feel sorry for her. I want to think her lifestyle was terrible, but everything in the Polo ad looks so nice.

I look through the pictures without speaking. Each picture takes me five minutes, and I take fewer and fewer glances back at the real Allie. Until we get to the swimsuit shot. "Oh my god," I say, "you had that body?"

"No. I didn't. I was standing in between two posts and lifting my arms as high as I could, and I twisted my torso to stretch my stomach. Right after that picture, I got a cramp in my back."

"Where are the other swimsuit shots?"

"This is the only one." She tells me she needed more swimsuit shots for her portfolio, so she found a photographer who also needed swimsuit shots in his portfolio, and he took photos of her.

"So where are they?" I ask.

"Would you wait? I'm getting there," she says. She says they went to this island near Tokyo, where she was working, and the guy told her she needed to loosen up, so he gave her a massage and he rubbed his penis against her back until he came. Allie's looking down when she tells me, and if I had ever seen Allie cry I'd worry she was going to cry now. But Allie never cries.

She goes out to her balcony and screams as loud as she can.

Someone yells back from the street, "Shut up, you crazy bitch."

"WHAT DO YOU WANT him to say?"

"I want him to tell me that I'm beautiful."

"Andy, do you think she's beautiful?"

"Yeah."

"Can you say it in a sentence?"

"Yeah, I think she's beautiful."

"Okay, but say it to her, not me."

"Okay, I think you're beautiful."

"Oh. That was really meaningful."

"What does Andy have to say to make it meaningful?"

"I don't know. Look, it's really depressing that it's so fucking difficult for him."

"Then why don't you tell him why this is so important to you."

"Oh my god. I can't believe this. How can he have sex with me if I'm not attractive to him? How can this not be totally obvious? This is so degrading to have to beg for compliments."

"I think if Andy understood your feelings then he would be more apt to express his own."

"Because if I'm not dating, and I'm not modeling, then my prettiness isn't worth anything if it doesn't turn Andy on. I mean, I'm getting ripped off. I feel unappreciated, like I'm not getting as much attention as I could be. If I give up seducing other men, then I have to at least know I have power over Andy. If he'd just tell me I'm beautiful, I'd feel it."

"I think that's why I don't want to tell her."

I PRETEND DAD AND I are husband and wife. "Honey," he asks, "what size are you?" "Sweetie," I say, "I'm a ten." He says that with my new breasts I'm probably a twelve. I put my arm around his waist while he picks out dresses that he likes. We have all twelves when the saleslady asks us if she can put the dresses in a fitting room. I wonder if the saleslady can tell I'm just a daughter. To throw her off, I slip my arm into his.

I tell him I'm going to the bathroom.

"I'll meet you back here," he says.

"No," I say, and touch his thigh, "I want you to come with me." He follows me. The sign for the bathrooms says left. I go right, through the stocking section.

"What're we doing here?" he asks. I slide my hand into his and give it a tug. Then I drop it and he follows me. I go to the shoe section without turning around and when I stop to look at a shoe he's right there behind me.

At the bathroom, I go in and he waits outside.

The saleslady says she wasn't sure if we were coming back. "Let me show you where the dressing room is," she says to me, "and you can come out here to show your dad."

"I'll just go in with her," Dad says.

When Dad sits down in the dressing room he looks so silly—the chair is too small, and he doesn't know what to do with his hands. He has this dumb smile on his face, like he's waiting for me to do something. I stand over him looking through the dresses. They're all strapless. I've never had a strapless dress before, and I'm thrilled, but I want to look mature, so I don't show my excitement.

"Stand up and unbutton me," I tell him, turning my back toward him. I've seen my mom do this a million times. But the only thing I have to unbutton is the top of my skirt. He does it, and then he unzips it, and the skirt falls while he slips his hands under my turtleneck, and lifts it over my head. I turn around in my bra and underwear and look at him. He looks at me. I know he wants to touch my breasts because he looks at them so often. So I lift his hand and put it on my breast before he can do it himself, so he knows I'm the one in charge.

It amazes me how childish he becomes with his hand on my breast. "Thank you," he says. "That's nice of you," he whispers. No one else can hear.

"Take off my bra," I whisper, as meanly and condescendingly as possible. And he listens to me. He unclasps the bra from the front. It falls to my shoulders, and I let it drop to the ground, and I stand there in front of him. I know he wants to touch my breasts again, but he's waiting for permission. This amazes me. I never want this moment to end. "No," I say, and push him back down in the chair. I lean over him to get a dress on the hook next to his head. I put my breasts in his face, but I don't let him touch.

I pull on a short, satin black dress. It's very tight, and I tell Dad to stand up and zip me. He does. I spin around the room while he stands there, with an awkward smile. "You look beautiful," he says.

I feel sophisticated.

The saleswoman knocks. "Is everything okay?" she asks.

"Yes, thank you for asking," I say, just like my mom.

While my dad recuperates in the chair, I manage to unzip myself.

I put on a pink, lacy dress, with a short full bottom. "Zip me," I say. He zips me and stands there. "Do you like it?" I ask.

"Yes," he says, staring at my breasts. "You look so innocent." And then he looks up at my eyes, and slowly moves toward me.

He thinks I'm going to move away, but I want to show him that I'm not scared of anything anymore, so I stand there, and he moves his head closer and closer, until his lips are on mine, and his tongue is in my mouth. I've done this before, with boys, and I want to make sure Dad can tell that I know what I'm doing. I move my tongue with his, and wrap my arms around him. I press my breasts against him, and he moans softly.

Then I bite his tongue. Hard, so it bleeds.

"Ow!" He says. He moves his head away from me. "What's wrong?" he says.

I'm silent for a few seconds, thinking. I move my arms across his back and up to his head. "I don't ever want to see you do this with Mom again. Do you understand?"

He understands.

ANDY AND I do one of those long weekend getaways to Palm Springs. The condo is Allie's mother's, and I think she uses it about once a year, because it's stale: puke green, over-exposed peach, and reprocessed air-conditioned air. Andy thinks "get away" means get away from any standard of cleanliness, so the place will look like a frat house in a few hours.

We read for most of the day. First Andy reads the three multimedia magazines he brought, and leaves them in the living room on the floor. Then he reads *Details*, because the cover article is about alternative music, and he leaves it on the bed. I don't say anything because he tries really hard not to be a slob when we're at home. I do tell him that catching up on work-related reading is not a vacation, and he says that what he reads is his business. Then he starts reading this book, *Fuzzy Thinking*, which I like because it seems like a less authoritarian view of science, and therefore a new possibility for the fertilizing of Andy's late-blooming feminism.

I read *The Ragged Way People Fall Out Of Love*, and keep interrupting Andy with pieces of information about what we have to do to keep from breaking up when we have teenage kids like the people in my book are doing—like, we can't always be too tired for each other. All Andy gets out of this is that I'm talking about kids and we're not even married, and this makes him think that I think we're married, and he thinks because he's said this to me before that I think I don't need to mention kids anymore, but I don't think that. "Don't worry," I tell him, "This is just informative."

"That's not what I was thinking," he says. "I'm thinking that you obsessing about how long our relationship is going to last is not a vacation." He smiles. I smile.

We read some more. I've had boyfriends who accused me of being boring when I wanted to stay home and read. They would accuse Andy of being boring too.

Our view from the rancid living room is the sterile golf course—hole eight. There are other condos across the green, and they all look the same—not just architecture, but the gardening—to the point where things don't look real. The exceptions are the pools, which come up every five houses in different and surprising shapes, like a diamond and a star.

I bring a beach ball, and devise a game where you bounce the beach ball off your head and try to make it drop on the other person's side of the front yard. I make up the rules as we go along, but Andy plays anyway. Sometimes, when he thinks I'm cheating, he'll make up his own counter-rule. Andy is a particularly bad athlete—he does things like step with his back foot when he swings a bat—so I was worried that any game I made up, Andy would be too uncoordinated to play, but he develops a way to bounce the ball off his head really hard, so that it drops too fast for me to catch, and he wins.

Andy makes dinner. He makes some sort of not-too-fishy-tasting fish, and broccoli because he knows I like it. We eat late, so the temperature has dropped 15 degrees to 100. We dine by candlelight, and attract zillions of bugs, which shouldn't even exist in the desert, but the whole climate changes with all the golf course watering.

For dessert, Andy whips up some gooey lime sauce for our ice cream cones, and he suggests we sit out by the pool—where we lick and we laugh dripping in lime, dangling toes in the blue.

"BOOKSHOP."

"Hello. I am calling you to inquire if you would perhaps be interested in buying some fictitious books?"

"We only buy real books."

"Okay. Thank you anyway."

MARC AND I like to play Risk, because the prospect of taking over the world is so luscious. Dad hates the game because it takes so long, but Mom brought it to Jamaica with us, "Just in case we have an emergency."

This is the third day in a row of rain on our relax-in-the-sun vacation. Dad agrees to play Risk to take his mind off the fact that he paid extra to get a room with 600 square feet of deck.

After two hours of intense play, and eight slices of banana cream pie from room service, the world is divided: Marc has Australia, Mom has North America, Dad has South America and I have Africa.

It's Dad's turn, and he wants to attack North Africa from Brazil. I start to cry. I try not to, but it's taken me two hours to get a continent.

Dad says, "Oh Christ. This is why I hate this game."

"I just got a continent," I say.

"Look," Dad says, "someone has to conquer everyone else. Someone has to win the game."

"But why North Africa? Why don't you take Mexico? Mom's got more armies than I do."

"Because that's not my plan," Dad says.

"It's not fair," I say, "look at Marc. He's got *all* of *Australia*, and no one's bothering him."

"He's too far away," Dad says. "And besides, I've got you on one side of me and Mom on the other. I have to attack one of you, or I won't get a card at the end of my turn. It's just how the game goes."

I cry. Dad has twenty-eight armies on Brazil, and I have three armies on North Africa.

I say, "I don't want to play."

ALLIE'S at a Zen Buddhist monastery. She wanted me to go with her, but I didn't want to take a week off from work—I want to buy a new mountain bike. It costs eighty dollars a night to stay there, or you can work for room and board—another reason not to go.

There is no one to read Kathy Acker out loud to.

There is no one to sand sit and body surf with when the air is hot and the water is warm in the middle of the day when we are not supposed to be at the beach because we care about our skin.

There is no one who calls me up to go out even though she knows I'm busy.

I am not busy. I am busy missing Allie.

She calls after three days. I know it's Allie before I hear her voice, because the operator wants me to sign my name somewhere in blood because Allie is calling me the most expensive way possible.

"What are you doing there?" I ask. "Do you hate it? Do you want to come home?"

"I love it. I miss you. Do you miss me? I want to be sure you miss me."

ALLIE TELLS ME she meditates five hours a day and works six. She cleans rooms. She used to collect stones, but she got fired because she kept making eyes at the head stone-collector monk. "They're all so adorable," she says. Now she's cleaning rooms. "The more expensive the room, the more garbage they generate." I think Allie thinks that if you clean enough of those rooms you learn what garbage looks like.

MRS. ZAK is my Hebrew school teacher. Mrs. Zak is saying, "A v with a dot inside is a b." No one is listening. Barry Rosenthal raises his hand, and says we can't concentrate today because last night the Brady Bunch got stuck in Hawaii, and we need to leave class early so we don't miss the beginning of tonight's episode.

We are all embarrassed for Barry's bad behavior. But we are quietly waiting for Mrs. Zak's answer.

Mrs. Zak is quietly waiting, too. She is looking at us.

She tells us to close our books, and she passes out licorice to the class. This is a big deal, because you can't make the guttural sounds with food in your mouth.

Then she tells us she was at Auschwitz. She says she will tell us a story about it. She folds her hands on top of her desk, and she tells us from the beginning, from the time when she was a fifth grader, like us. She tells us her mother didn't let go of her hand for three days. That's how scared her mother was of being separated. But they were separated anyway, and Mrs. Zak never saw her mother again. I think about if I never saw my mother again, and I can't believe Mrs. Zak isn't crying. Her hands are shaking, though.

She says if you don't tell stories, people can pretend it never happened. I think that even though she yells at us for not doing our homework, she likes us because she is letting us see her shake. I want to do something nice for Mrs. Zak, like do my homework every week. But I know I can't do that, so I decide to be a person who holds stories.

She lets us touch her tattoo, and it is black and bumpy. Then she lets us out of class early.

I USE THE FLOWERED PATTERN first. The blood dyes the fabric a deep maroon, but the little flowers stay white. I experiment with different ways to fold the fabric when I put it in my vagina because each fold gives a unique, tye-died effect.

Allie's squares are a lighter red than mine. She takes out her squares sooner than I do, so her's have some white on the sides.

I dry my squares on my balcony.

Andy says the squares smell and they're attracting ants.

I tell him this is a way to celebrate menstruation and to show respect for the beauty of my blood.

Andy says he'll take me out to dinner tonight.

Allie and I are disappointed when the bleeding stops, but we have enough squares to start a quilt.

While Andy reads *Rolling Stone* on the sofa, Allie and I arrange the squares in a pattern on the kitchen floor. Andy points out that the fabric is hardening, and the squares with a lot of blood are getting sort of crusty, crumbling on the floor.

Allie and I look at him.

"I mean," he says, "that maybe you should rinse them out. Like pre washed jeans, you know, to get out the excess dye."

We wash the squares and almost all the blood comes out.

"Blood never comes out of anything," Allie says. "This is amazing."

Andy suggests that we make some bed sheets out of the fabric.

Instead, we rip out the cotton lining in our underwear, and we reline it with our stainless, white-on-white, flowered fabric.

Andy says we look like a sewing bee. Then he mops up the floor.

"WHAT ARE YOU?" I asked on my first date with Andy.

"Nothing," he said. I took that as a good thing—not Jewish, but not anything mutually exclusive to Jewish. So we could continue dating.

I felt the need to convince myself that I could just convert him—then we could celebrate Jewish holidays together and our kids could grow up Jewish and our lives would have spiritual meaning. I started out trying to logically convince him that the only true way for him to be spiritual was through organized religion, and the best one was Judaism. Andy laughed, but when I gave him a fuck you look, he collected himself and suggested I explain to him why Judaism was spiritual to me.

I bought lots of books to compose a logical explanation. But every time I tried to explain Judaism to Andy, the task seemed too big, and I got frustrated. And when it didn't feel too big, it felt too embarrassing—like prayers that refer to God as "King of the Universe."

So I stopped dealing with the whole religion issue. But then I started to feel lost and lonely on Jewish holidays, and I started to hate Andy for not being Jewish and now I'm wishing he were a fanatic Catholic so I could just dump him.

"WHAT ABOUT ANDY?" Allie asks. I look back, and Andy is bobbing on his boogie board in between eight-year-olds in water up to his knees.

"Leave him there," I say. "He won't wear his glasses in the water, so he can't see. He won't come out this far."

"He won't get any waves."

"He doesn't want any."

Allie paddles out to me and we lie on our stomachs on our boards. The first big wave knocks me over, and I have to chase my board. Allie shows me that if you don't want to take a big wave, you flip yourself under your board and hold on.

When we crash back to shore, Andy tells us we're going out farther than we need to.

We paddle back out, even farther, side by side, flipping ourselves under like synchronized swimmers.

The waves are breaking more and more unevenly and we float for a while, waiting for a good one, until we hear a lifeguard yelling something on a megaphone and motioning with his arms.

He is good-looking—even while flapping.

Soon his too-tan body is on a lifeguard board and he is yelling for us to come in. He is yelling, "Riptide!"

"What's that," I ask Allie.

"It's what surfers die in."

We don't budge. We figure we'll catch a wave rather than paddle all the way in.

Before we get a wave, we get the lifeguard at our feet, telling us to go back before the currents make it impossible.

Allie paddles her mouth to my ear. "He likes us," she says.

While he goes off to reel in other boogie boarders, we paddle very very slowly. He comes back to see if we need help. We giggle and water gets in my nose and I start coughing. Allie falls off her board—maybe a little too dramatically—and the lifeguard holds her board while she climbs back on. He says he'll pull her in. I want to fall off my board too, but I am not as well-trained an actress as Allie, so I have to settle for Andy, who is waiting on the shore.

THE WHOLE FAMILY is in the kitchen trying to find something to eat. I just got my driver's license and we thought Mom was going to make dinner for us, to celebrate, but everyone wants something we don't have, so she makes herself a Scotch and water. I settle for Velveeta cheese. Dad has mint chip ice cream. Marc tries to make himself a Slurpee in the blender, but it's a lot crunchier than he expected, so he has nothing.

Mom knows she disappointed us with dinner so she suggests we play Scrabble. Dad and I agree immediately, because we always want a chance to beat Mom. Marc hates Scrabble—he's not a words person—but the only time I can win is when he plays: Mom and Dad make two- and three-letter words that get lots of points and don't leave space to make anything but more two- and three-letter words. Marc always sits next to me, and sacrifices his turn with words like R-U-L-E-R, which is only worth five points but pokes out in the board and gives me lots of good letters to work with. I convince Marc to play by telling him I'll sit in his bedroom and listen to the money clink on the Pink Floyd record. He says he'll play if I'll also drive him to seven-eleven to get a Slurpee.

The only time we talk is to challenge. Dad challenges Mom on "eth." "Dad," Marc says, "don't challenge her. You know she's memorized the whole *Scrabble Dictionary*."

"Dad, do it," I say. I kick Marc under the table. Marc and I can only benefit from this challenge—either Mom loses a turn or Dad loses a turn.

Dad looks at Mom, looks for signs. "Well," he says, "I'll just try it."
He looks up eth: Archaic, third person singular present.

"That'll teach you to challenge me," Mom says, and collects her
thirty-eight points.

Mom wins. Now Mom's in the mood to make us all what we
want for dinner. But now Marc and I are driving to seven-eleven.

The official story is someone must have hit the car in the seven-
eleven parking lot while we were buying Slurpees. Marc is really
nervous that there will be a big fight at home, but he has to tell the
story because I know I'd laugh, or say something like the truth,
which is that I was frantically searching the radio stations when I hit
a fire hydrant. I don't want Mom and Dad to take away my license,
but I don't show my nervousness to Marc—he can barely compose
himself as it is.

"You'll be great," I tell him, on the drive home. "I'll be right
there next to you, for moral support."

"Will you turn down the radio? Can you at least pay attention on
the drive home?" he says.

"I was paying attention."

"I'm so sick of you pissing off Mom and Dad."

"I'm sick of you never pissing them off."

We don't say anything else. We know we can't be angry at each
other when we get home; Mom and Dad wouldn't know what to do
so they'd overreact about the car.

We go into the house calmly, and I stand close to Marc while he
tells the story. At first, Dad isn't angry, but then Mom sees he's not
angry, and she gets angry at him, because she'll have to drive us to
school until the car gets fixed. Then Dad gets angry at us so Mom
can stop being angry at him.

Marc says we'll walk to school for a week, and I glare at him, but he glares back harder with a pleading glare, like, I just don't want a fight.

It's not like me to give in to Mom, but Marc has had a hard night already, so I agree to walk to school.

Then we go up to Marc's room, and we curl up on his red shag rug with the lights out, and we listen to Pink Floyd and watch the lights on the stereo. After three songs we still haven't said anything, so I say, "Marc, are we going to talk or just listen?"

"I don't care," he says.

I say, "I'm sorry about the fire hydrant."

He grunts.

I hate it when he gets like this because it makes me feel lonely, like he's somewhere else. But I don't want to leave him, because then he'd feel lonely too. So I listen to five sides of Pink Floyd until we've both fallen asleep with our heads in the carpet and the needle scratching in our ears.

WE HAVE SEX in the morning and I miss the bus, so Andy has to drive me to work.

I love when we have sex in the morning because in L.A., cool people do not take the bus.

When Andy drops me off, I accidentally leave *Tristram Shandy* in his car. I look for a new book to read, but I hate starting a new book before I've finished the last one. I need to feel like I'm getting stuff accomplished.

I call up Andy. "I left my book in your car."

"Oh," he says. "This morning?"

"Yeah," I say. I don't want to ask him to come back with it because that would be unreasonable.

He says, "I'll bring it by when I go to lunch, okay?"

"Well, when are you going to lunch?"

"I'll just bring it right now," he says.

In the bookstore I know everything and Andy knows nothing. He brings me the book and I put my arms around him.

He says, "I have to get back to work."

I should have known he wouldn't want to stay.

MY DAD AND I were sitting in the hospital—Northwestern's department of neurology. I was getting tested for dyslexia, or attention deficit syndrome, or, as my dad put it to the doctor, "Whatever you think might be appropriate."

I didn't mind this testing because I got out of a day at school, and I hadn't finished the chemistry lab that was due that day. Also, I'd have an interview with the neurologist, and I liked these kinds of interviews because I had been to so many head people that I could always impress them with succinct and insightful synopses of my life.

But the interview never happened. What happened was first, she interviewed my dad. It was long, and I got through two acts of *Macbeth*. Then my dad came out, and she called me into her office. "What are you reading?" she asked.

"*Macbeth*. It's the Folger edition because I like having the definitions," I told her. I always avoided one word answers with head people—they like long ones.

"Are you reading it for school?"

"No. We read *Romeo and Juliet* in school, and I really liked it, so I thought I'd read something else by Shakespeare." Just when I was gearing up to tell her my life story, she called my dad in to join us.

She told him that I seemed fine to her, and she wasn't sure why he wanted me tested. My dad told her that the family had been having lots of problems with me, and he didn' t know what to do. He started crying, so of course, she asked me to leave the room.

I read two more acts and then the tests began.

She laid me down on a table and put Vaseline in my hair. Then she put all kinds of discs on my hair so that there were cords coming out of a machine and going into my head. It was exactly like *ET*, at the end of the movie, and I got excited about describing this to the kids at school.

I lay there for about five minutes and then it was over. We waited around a little longer, until the neurologist brought us into her office and told us that my results were fine.

My dad said, "Oh."

I said, "Can I have a copy of the results to show my homeroom teacher? Because my dad wrote a note to excuse me from school today, but the day I stayed home because the police were there, my dad lied to my teacher, and she found out, so I need some kind of proof that I was at the hospital today."

I DECIDE I'LL BE the super secure new girlfriend, and I say, Sure, Ann can stay with us. A week? Two? Sure. After all, she's the one who got dumped, and I'm the one webbed in between Andy's flannel sheets. I make sure I look hot when she gets here—not the dressed-up-for-you hot, but the I'm-so-good-looking-I-don't-have-to-try hot—which takes me a hair hour in the morning, and six changes of clothes during the day.

I decide she's cute, but not as muscular as I am, and not as tall, and not as smart. Andy picked her in a moment of desperation, before he ever dreamed of being with someone like me.

I befriend her.

While Andy's at work, we swap tales of his bed performance. She tells tales of impotence, which I've heard from Andy. I tell her he gets it up fine for me; I don't say it braggingly because I don't have to. I tell her our problem is that I have to ask him a billion times a month to go down on me, and he does it like it's a fucking favor. I know he never went down on Ann, but she tells me anyway. "I know," I say.

We make Andy cook dinner for us, while we tease him about all the shitty senseless things he did to Ann when they were dating. Like, she went on a backpacking trip for two weeks, and he rented her his tent, which he neglected to tell her had four leaks. "I didn't know myself," he says, sticking his head in the oven.

"I feel really bad about how I treated you, Ann," he says later, while we're all drinking wine.

Ann thanks him for the apology.

She's good-looking, in an apple pie sort of way, and I tell Andy I really want to have her in bed with us. I tell him it's so weird and arbitrary that she slept in his bed when they had the couple label and now we have the label so I'm in the bed and she's out. I shudder to think of myself as the next one on the floor.

He says no way.

I want to fuck her. I want her to be mine, and not just Andy's.

I whisper into his ear a story about how she gets in bed with us and I play with his nipples and kiss him while she sucks on his penis, and when she feels precum in her mouth, she gets really excited, and I go down on her from behind while she's sucking, and Andy says that's an unappealing scene and he'd rather just be with me.

Dinner conversation is about how Andy and Ann fucked in a forest and the ranger came. Andy and I have never done that. They are laughing. I am laughing, too.

In bed I am moping, face in pillow, naked, hoping to fall asleep even though it's too early.

Andy asks why I'm in bed.

I bolt up dramatically and say, "I can't believe you talked about fucking each other in front of me."

"I didn't know it would bother you. It wasn't planned. I didn't mean to. I hadn't even remembered until she brought it up."

"Why didn't you just fuck, right there with the silverware?" I hiss. I want to yell, but Ann would hear.

"Because I don't want to fuck her. And she's not interested either, and you know that."

"Can't you see how hurtful that was?"

"No. Can you explain it to me?"

"What? No, I can't explain it to you. How can this need explaining? How would you feel if I were reminiscing with the married man in front of you?"

"But you do. You tell me about him all the time, and I don't feel jealous."

"I am not jealous. Ann is an idiot. You are a pompous ass for thinking I'm jealous. You want that. You want us to compete."

Andy is quiet. He gets quiet when he thinks I'm attacking him. He thinks the quiet will get me to stop. He is sitting on the bed, fully clothed, waiting for this to happen. I am quiet. Quietly naked and pulling the covers up to my shoulders trying to disappear.

"I feel insecure," I tell him, and pull the covers over my head.

I peek out for a second, to make sure he's still there. He looks sad, he looks down, he asks what he can do.

"I want to feel special," I tell him. I look away.

"Do you want me to ask her to leave? I'll do that. I'll tell her she can't stay with us next time she's in town either."

"Thank you," I say. I go back under the covers before he can kiss me. But I leave my forehead uncovered so he can try again.

I BEGIN READING BOOKS on tracking ovulation. Andy is skeptical. He says he is willing to wear a condom, but I appeal to the granola side of him, and tell him it'll make us more in touch with nature. The best information comes from Catholic organizations, and from that I learn to stick my finger up my vagina and learn how to find my cervix. I wipe off a mucus sample every morning. I also learn to chart my morning temperature.

After a few months I can tell when I'm pre ovulatory, when I'm ovulating, and when I'm done. I'm not very good with the temperature chart, because as soon as I wake up I crawl all over Andy, which makes my temperature artificially high. But I keep a calendar on my wall that has twenty-nine days in the shape of a circle, and every day I write down the status of my mucus.

I love my mucus.

Andy worries because he never knows where we are in the cycle, and he just has to trust me. "Look," I say, "the worst that'll happen is I'll get pregnant."

"Well, that's pretty bad."

"Then you keep track with me."

I draw a circle calendar in his day runner, in the important accounts section, and every day I call up his assistant to update Andy's calendar with mucus adjectives.

Six month later I get pregnant. It's a similar feeling to the first time I used my hand to make a boy ejaculate; I couldn't believe it really worked.

I scout around for abortion places, and I pick an expensive one since Andy's paying. We do a drive-by so we know how to get there, and Evangelists have surrounded the place with Bibles and placards and noise.

I look forward to plowing through the people the next morning, but the next morning there are no political outbursts to distract me, and in the waiting room I start imagining the procedure.

"Andy," I say, "do you want to play the state game while we wait?"

"What?"

"The game where I say a state and you have to say a state that begins with the last letter of the state I said."

"No. I don't feel like that now."

"Well what are we going to do while we wait?"

"I don't know."

I can tell other games will not interest him either.

We wait. I start thinking about what it would be like to have a baby. We wait a half hour. There are complications with the woman before me. I start imagining all the combinations of complications I could have that would lead to death. Andy assures me that the percentages of death are minuscule.

Andy starts imagining the combinations of complications that could lead to me not getting the abortion. I know this is what he's imagining because he keeps saying, "I know this is hard, but at least we know it'll be over today. At least we know it'll be over today."

The nurse tells us I'll have to make another appointment because the doctor has to stay with this other woman.

I am relieved. I want to go home and think about the baby. On the drive home, Andy says he's worried that I won't get an abortion. "Don't worry," I tell him, "I'll kill it."

"It's not a person," he says. "When you say things like that, I get worried. It's not a person."

I feel like I've done this so many times.

"We need to make another appointment as soon as we get home."

"I can't do this again. I'm so tired of purging people from my life."

"This is not a person."

"DON'T FUCKING TELL ME WHAT I HAVE INSIDE ME."

We are quiet the rest of the way home. Andy runs a red light.

Andy wants to make an appointment as soon as we get home. I ignore him, and go into the bedroom shutting the door behind me. I don't want to be alone, but being with Andy makes me feel lonely. I fall asleep with my hands on my stomach.

When I wake up it's dark, and I feel like I've missed something, but I can't say what. I think about my friend whose mom wanted an abortion but didn't have the money. I press on my stomach, and I know there's something there, but I don't feel it. I lie in bed listening for Andy, trying to figure out what he's doing, where he is. In between sounds, I think about not having the abortion; I want something inside me. I want to stop putting stuff in and ripping it out. But I try to imagine life with me, Andy, and a baby, and I can only see Andy leaving.

I call Andy into the bedroom, and he comes in slowly, like the door's rigged. I tell him to sit on the edge of the bed, and I tell him to make an appointment for tomorrow morning. "But this is it," I tell him. "I'm not aborting anything else, so I want to be really careful. Condom, diaphragm, this will be a lot of work." Andy nods an I-love-you nod. I hold his hand tightly.

I WANT TO GO to graduate school, but I failed fifty percent of my classes senior year of college so I don't have anyone to write me recommendations. I sign up for a writing class at a community college. The teacher there likes me so much that we do lunch every Wednesday. We talk about books we've read. I read D.H. Lawrence and Elizabeth McNeil because I notice my teacher is most impressed with my sexual insight. He reads Cervantes and Sir Walter Scott, so I think he thinks I'm impressed with size.

I tell my therapist I can't concentrate on making myself a better person because I'm short two recommendations. My therapist says this is his day job, and he's really a screenwriter, and he can recommend me. I am skeptical. He says he's written TV movies and directed lower-than-TV movies, and that's good enough for me.

I tell Andy I can't have sex because I'm short a recommendation, and that makes me feel insecure about what I'm doing with my life, and I can't be intimate when I feel insecure. Andy says I should use one of my past employers, which is a stupid idea because graduate schools don't care how well you operate a cash register. I tell him I have a better idea.

I tell Andy to say I was vice president of his company, but he says I should let him write what he wants. I say, Okay, but he must include the following tidbits about me: Creative genius, intellectual powerhouse, easy-to-get-along-with. He also has to fill out the form that says this person is in the top one-percent, five-percent, or ten-percent etc., of likely candidates. I tell Andy to check off top one percent. He says they'll know he's my lover. I say he won't be my lover if he doesn't do it.

In the final draft of the letter he writes that I am the most well-read person he knows, and I'm really touched, even though the rest of the people he knows are L.A. types.

I give Andy the confidential envelope for his recommendation. I take the original and put it in a box with love letters from old boyfriends.

THIS IS THE END—my last day of therapy. It's sad to look at my therapist's dopey clothes and graying hair because I've spent so many hours looking at them that they seem to show my reflection.

It shouldn't be scary to leave the therapist, because I'm not sick. But if I'm not sick, what am I? If I'm not in therapy, where will I be?

"In Boston," the therapist tells me. I can tell he's proud that he's gotten rid of another client.

DAVID SAYS the fumes from the paint are so strong, they're leaking to the hall, and if I don't stop painting soon, there will be a permanent stench.

"Do you like it?" I say. "It's the beach."

"Sand on the ceiling?"

"No," I say, "that's the sun, and the blue on the wall is the ocean."

"Do you want to have dinner with me?" David asks, "I made lots of pasta."

"Your walls are green," I tell him.

"Yeah. They came that way. These are the beaches on Mars. Do you like lots of sauce?"

David says, "That woman who sits in the corner of our Thursday class keeps putting her hand up her shirt."

"I saw that too," I say.

ANDY CALLS ME to say everything is going into his business. "I owe so much," he says. His Gold Card is running out of steam.

He says he sold his Porsche, and bought a Volkswagen, and it's killing him.

I tell him the Volkswagen is way cooler than the Porsche. I tell him driving a Porsche is like screaming that you are so insecure you need people to admire you because of your car.

Andy says he feels numb driving the Volkswagen; he feels closer to the transmission when he drives the Porsche.

I say, I love that he bought a Volkswagen because it meets California requirements for smog emissions.

But I really like the Volkswagen because we can talk about it instead of talking about our feelings. Or we can talk about our feelings about the Volkswagen, and we can give ourselves credit for talking about feelings.

I SPENT last Rosh Hashanah in California body surfing. I was embarrassed to be seen traveling, which is strictly forbidden, so I walked three miles on side streets to a secluded beach.

This year, I decide to go back to Illinois for Rosh Hashanah. I don't tell Andy why. I don't know why. The week before Rosh Hashanah, Dad calls, in a bonding mood because I am willing to be Jewish again. In a fit of trust, I tell him Andy is not meeting me in Illinois. "I saw this coming," Dad says. He thinks leaving Andy back in Los Angeles means breakup is imminent, followed by a journey back to Illinois—with all my belongings—to find a nice Jewish boy.

This smugness makes me sick. Before I leave, I have Allie send me some black-sequined, white-feathered, only-in-Hollywood clothes to shock my family at Rosh Hashanah.

I fly into Chicago two hours before sundown. Dad picks me up at baggage claim. I toss my luggage into the backseat and get in the car.

We say hi to each other. He knows not to kiss me hello.

We talk about the weather: Cold. We talk about the family: Marc is living in an ivory tower with an Israeli girlfriend. We talk about the route my dad is taking home because it looks crooked to me.

"We're late," my dad says, "We're going straight to synagogue."

"But these are flying clothes," I say.

"You can change in the car."

My face gets red and my body tightens. My ears ring, but my voice is silent. He's apologized a million times for everything he's ever done. I can't keep complaining.

I don't want to be quiet for too long, because I don't want him to know something's wrong. I say, "I'll just wear pants to synagogue."

"People will think you're crazy," he says.

"Well let's stop at a gas station and I'll change."

"No," he says, "there's no time."

The rest of the drive we say nothing.

We're late to synagogue, but we get to go right to the front of the seating area because my parents give so much money. The place is packed because everyone who ever goes to synagogue goes on Rosh Hashanah to celebrate the Jewish new year. I kiss Marc and Mom hello, and take a seat between Dad and Marc. Marc squeezes my hand and whispers, "I'm never coming with them again—they've been fighting all day."

"What?" I ask with a smile, "what were they fighting about?"

"Dad wanted to write our names in the prayer book so no one would steal them, and Mom said writing counts as work and you can't work on Rosh Hashanah." We both laugh.

I look in my prayer book, and my name is not in it.

"I've missed you," I tell him. The service begins with familiar songs that fill the synagogue, and Marc and I sway as we pray. We recite the prayers like memorized poems that live inside us, and even though I don't believe God is a man, I recite, He is the Lord our God, because it's so deep inside me. And when it comes to my lips, it is big and loud and brings out all the other parts of me it lives with.

I stand patiently, feeling the ache of these words, and following in the prayer book until my father drops his book, and it thuds on the floor and lands at my feet. I lose my place as I bend down to pick up the book, and he bends down too, and our heads knock down by our feet, and my prayer book falls. Another thud. My book is too far under the seat in front of me to reach. Dad picks up his prayer book and kisses it, and I see his fat red lips pucker, press and smack.

At that moment my prayers are gone; I cannot stand next to my father and pray from his book, to his god. I walk out of synagogue. I take a cab to the airport and fly back to Boston on Rosh Hashanah. I leave my baggage behind, in my father's car.

DAVID IS IN HIS KITCHEN making a strawberry sandwich. I ask for one. Then I realize I don't want a sandwich. "David," I say, "I'm premenstrual."

"Does this have something to do with the sandwich, or is it separate?"

"I just want you to know that I'm sensitive now. It's the week before my period."

"The *week*?" he asks.

"Be nice to me or I'll cry."

David shakes his head and hands me a sandwich. Then he takes the sandwich back, and says, "I'll take the greens off yours since you're sensitive."

ALLIE SAYS I'm too self-absorbed to be a good friend.

"Give me an example," I tell her.

"Your letters," she says. "You write letters like you're talking to a wall. You write them like I'm not there. No, like I am there, to listen to you go on and on about your life."

"Allie, I thought 'How are you?' would be trite."

"Well it's not. It's a common sentiment for people who give a shit about someone besides themselves."

Until now, I thought of myself as a good letter writer. I tell Allie I'll think about it and I'll call her back. "Thank you for sharing your feelings with me," I say.

"Don't dish out that therapy crap to me," she says, and hangs up.

▼

DAVID TAKES ME to a party in the South End. The room is divided into a men's side and a women's side. I ask him if it's because they are Orthodox Jews. "No," he says, "they're gay."

Ten minutes later, David has disappeared, but a woman has taken his place.

She asks me if I'm a lesbian, or did I just come here with David.

I take some pizza puffs off the hors d'oeuvre table and look around at the other people at the party. I can't decide what to say.

I assess my chances of being able to maintain the lie if I say I'm a lesbian.

I examine her—try to decide if she is someone I would like to sleep with.

I try to figure out what she wants to hear, what she expects to hear, what I want to be, and I try to find something in between.

"I don't know," I say.

But I don't like saying I don't know. I know she is a lesbian and I've read enough women-seeking-women ads to know real lesbians don't fuck experimenters. So I say, "I don't really like how I am with men."

But then I think maybe she will think I'm just a poser. I say, "When I've been with a woman, there's been an equality I have never had with a man." This implies that I'm with women all the time.

Five seconds have passed.

The woman is munching on party food. She offers me some celery. I take some, hoping this will bond us.

I tell her I want to hang out with lesbians. I say everything short of Please be my friend. Wait, no, I pretty much say that too. This is what I want: To become friends with a group of lesbians, and they

▶

will be so attracted to me that even though I'm not a purebred, a (very tall and very breasted) lesbian will seduce me, and the moment will be so equal—so clean of power—that it won't even count as cheating on Andy.

"LIKE, I COULD SAY, I'm sucking on your breasts and rolling your nipples around on my tongue."

"Stop. Don't say that," I tell Andy.

"Try one sentence. I'm rubbing my face across your stomach, licking your belly button, and now I'm going lower."

"Okay," I say, "Okay, here's a sentence . . . I'm putting in my diaphragm."

Andy laughs. I feel like a geek.

"And then what?"

"Why don't we practice when you visit? I need to see your face and be touching you when we do this. I need to practice first."

"Yeah."

"I could get really drunk and call you back in half an hour."

"Okay," he says. He hangs up. I can't believe he's agreeing to this. It seems like so far to go just to have phone sex. I've already used up eight dollars talking about not being able to talk.

I start thinking about turning Andy on with what I say. We're both too inhibited to say stuff while we're fucking. I imagine his penis inside me and him talking to me about my breasts, and phone sex dialogue starts rolling through my head.

I take sips of whiskey and practice out loud, in whispers, so no one can hear: "I'm reaching for your penis." But then I wonder if I should say cock. I've never said cock. It seems crass. Then I go upstairs. I feel good because I trip twice.

I wait fifteen more minutes. I have a few pieces of leftover lasagna. I fold the rest of my laundry. I have some more lasagna. I feel dizzy. I go upstairs, and pee on the way to my bedroom. I bring the phone into my bedroom, shut the door, and put a towel over the crack. I get naked.

"Hi," I say. "I'm ready."

"How much did you drink?"

I say, "Don't be telling me I didn't drink the right stuff or something. What are you doing right now?"

"I'm lying in bed. Naked," he says.

Usually, when I masturbate, I use just one finger so it's not messy, but this time, I use all my fingers. I come the same way I would if Andy's fingers were there—lots of orgasms in a row. At the end, when Andy says he's coming, I come again.

"Good night," he tells me, "I love you."

"I'm falling asleep with my head on your chest and our legs intertwined," I say. After we hang up, I lie there in bed. But I have no afterglow. I feel sick. I feel like I'm going to feel sick tomorrow. So I go downstairs to the bathroom and throw up.

"HOW CAN YOU want to go to bookstores?" David asks. "You have to write the contemporary lit midterm."

"I wrote it already."

"You did not. You haven't even read the books."

"The books suck. I am not reading Annie Proulx. All the inanimate objects have feelings."

"Is that what you wrote?"

"No. I read the *New York Times Book Review* and wrote the paper from that."

"You're going to get thrown out of the program," he says more than once on our way to the bookstore.

I spend most of my time stealthily reorganizing. I move *One Hundred Years of Solitude* from the M's to the G's. I move *I Know Why the Caged Bird Sings* from fiction to autobiography.

Some guy has been watching me, and just as he starts to approach, David intercepts him, and calls out his name. They are friends from Provincetown. David introduces me.

The guy asks where I'm from, and I say L.A. He says I sound like I have a midwest accent.

I go back to reorganizing.

ALLIE CALLS. She read an article that says the relationships that last are relationships where people can get over arguments quickly.

I say I'll be back in L.A. for winter break really soon, and then she won't have to put up with my bad letters.

I DON'T TELL HIM that I love him. No one does. It's an unwritten rule, because one woman did, and we never saw her again. I don't tell him I love him, but he pulls the story out of a paragraph that I didn't know was his. And because he's not just my teacher, but my audience, too, I turn the paragraph in to him. When he says, "Make this longer," I have to show him that I take his advice.

He reads my paragraph before he goes home after class, and I'm wet with sweat watching him through the window. He sees me watching and motions with his hand for me to come back into the room, and then the two people whose mouths are full of words are full of each other's, and we are lovers.

The next week in class I feel special because when everyone is done reading their stories, I know I will be the story he concentrates on most.

I bring him back to the house and sneak him up to my bedroom, where I have carefully displayed casually all the details he needs to put my life together in the way I want him to. My details are perfect because he tells me I'm clever and stunning and did he ever tell me how lovely my eyes are. He doesn't notice I painted my walls to match my eyes. I lead him to bed right away—no artificial suspense.

But in bed, he is annoying, especially his tongue. I lift my head off the pillow and call down the bed to him: "Please, you can't focus on the clitoris—it'll never work. A vagina is like a story—you have to move around the edges, through the hair, under the flaps, with assurance and creativity. Don't go directly for what you want."

But he can't tell a story, he can only teach.

DAVID AND I are at Urban Outfitters buying trendy clothes. Clothes-shopping with David is like shopping with a boyfriend, but better because David takes a genuine interest. David is looking at boxers. "Why are you looking at boxers?" I ask. "You don't wear boxers."

"How would you know?" he says very loudly. And before I can say, Why are you yelling? I see that David is cruising in the Calvin Klein section and I am cramping his style.

IT'S THE SECOND WEEK of my winter vacation, and Andy is still covered with spots and he can't leave the apartment. The only thing we've done all week is entertain families who want to expose their kids to chicken pox.

I decide we have to bond somehow, because if we can't enjoy being with each other when I'm home, then there's nothing in the relationship to look forward to when I'm away at school.

I rent a movie, which astounds Andy because I don't have the attention span for movies. Andy's seen everything from the last thirty-five years because he's lived in L.A. his whole life, so I rent a Katherine Hepburn and Spencer Tracy movie. We settle into bed, and I curl up next to him, even though some of his pox are still full of puss. The movie is about Spencer Tracy's boring fiancée and his love for exciting Katherine Hepburn, which is the same as their real lives, so it bores me. I want to make out instead of watching, but Andy says he needs to get more scabs—he says contact hurts his open sores.

"Then we have to think of something else to do together," I say. "Time is ticking. I'm leaving soon." We decide to try talking to people on the Internet. We access Andy's e-world account, which we don't really know how to use. We get ourselves into a room, but the conversations are going too quickly to figure out what they're about. Someone types, "Hi, Andy," because that's Andy's log-in name. I type back, "Hi," but I have nothing else to say. No one says anything to me. I am figuring out that you have to have a catchy name, because Lois Lane, Dr. Cool and Gigit are all immersed in conversation.

I tell Andy he has to switch his name so people will talk to me. Andy tries, but it's too much work. So I go to the sex room as Andy, and it's full of men, and someone types in that they don't need any more men. I type back "I'm not Andy, I'm a woman," and the people in the room ignore me, and Andy is itching, so we turn off the computer and go to sleep.

"I'M NOT THE SEXUAL DYNAMO I used to be," I tell Andy, pushing his penis and everything attached to it away from me.

"Used to be?" he asks.

"Well, I used to be able to ignore my emotions and just fuck."

"Oh," he says, and takes his hand off my breast. "Do you want to talk?"

He rolls to my side and nuzzles his face in my neck. I turn over on my back to look at the ceiling.

I tell him, "I want to be passionate and loving, but I keep thinking about what I can do next to please you."

"What does that mean?" he says.

"I need time to think," I say.

Andy takes a shower. I put on a T-shirt and think in bed. I think I'm tired of bed. I'm tired of sex.

Andy gets out of the shower. "Let's go for a walk on the beach," I say.

We walk across the street to the steps down to the beach.

Waves crack against the steep slope, and our feet slap the sand while we hold hands. I ask Andy to walk on the sea side of me.

"Why?" he asks. "You don't like the waves?"

"No," I say, "it's not the waves. I feel like being taller than you."

ALLIE IS COMING over for dinner with her new boyfriend and I'm checking him out. This is the point. Andy thinks the point is to make a nice dinner; he is Martha Stewart with his sautéed mushrooms and green-olive sauce.

"I thought we were ordering pizza," I say from the kitchen doorway.

"I felt like cooking," he says, absorbed in his breading.

Rodrigo. Saying his name is torture—I can't roll my r's. Apparently, Allie called earlier to find out what to bring, and Andy said vegetables, and she brought a Hubbard squash the size of a football. "It needs to be cooked," she says. We both look at Andy; he takes the squash. Allie gives Rodrigo a look like, "Learn something from this."

At dinner Rodrigo says he's an aspiring director; he writes films. "About what?" I ask, being congenial because I promised, but thinking, Ugh, she might as well be with an actor.

He says he's making a romantic comedy

I pause, thinking he's making a joke. "Oh," I say. "How does this affect your soul?"

Allie spills water across the whole table.

Andy cleans up.

Rodrigo tells me the family in his romantic comedy is Italian and he's Italian-American.

I say, "Oh."

Allie gestures with a sautéed asparagus. She says that Rodrigo has a video of one of the movies she was in, before she stopped drinking and fucking producers. Rodrigo is not impressed. Allie gave him a Jeanette Winterson novel, and he's plodding through it even though it's not as linear as a romantic comedy. Rodrigo listens to me and Allie ranting about how Jeanette Winterson is redefining storytelling outside the patriarchal structure.

Andy listens, too.

❦

ALLIE IS GOING to the egg donor place because they pay $3,000 an egg, and Allie wants a PowerBook. I accompany her to see if this is something I could do, too.

She fills out a long form about her short life and they reject her. "Why?" Allie says angrily.

The nurse looks at Allie. "Miss," she says, "you have checked off alcoholism, mental illness, drug addiction, and felony in your family history."

"Oh, don't worry about that," Allie says, "it's all the same person. My dad is messy, but he's the only one."

Allie and I leave feeling like we lost $3,000. We console ourselves with empty omelets at Century City. "I should have lied," she says.

ANDY NEVER COMES over to my side of the bed, so I was really surprised when I woke up with him crawling on top of me and the earth rocking under me. Maybe he was thinking that his side of the bed was next to the huge bookcase that he was always going to nail to the wall tomorrow. Or maybe he was thinking that he wanted me awake to be terrified with him, but there wasn't time to think. We sat there on the shaking bed, naked, hugging. I knew I was going to die, and I was ready to go peacefully. I didn't notice it was dark and I didn't notice everything in our kitchen cabinets was falling onto the floor. I only felt Andy clinging to me for his life.

When the shaking stopped, I got our earthquake flashlight out from under the bed. I had seen pictures of the San Francisco earthquake, where sides of buildings fell, and all I could think of was Channel 7 broadcasting our bedroom while we were naked. I made my way to the closet, over fallen books and crumbled plaster. Everything was on the floor, so I took the first four shoes I could find, and an armload of clothing. Andy sat on the bed stunned. "Put this stuff on," I told him.

Then Andy wanted to see if our earthquake food was okay. He went to the kitchen, and I shined the flashlight onto the floor. "This place is trashed," I said, "we have to get out of here."

We went outside with our neighbors and listened to radios and watched fires burning all around us. When the sun came up we could see the cracks all over the building, and it didn't look safe to go back.

Andy and I go back.

We stand in our apartment, in the doorway. Everything that could have broken did.

Andy has this collection of junk that used to be his dad's, before his dad ditched the family for a younger woman. All the stuff is broken, and Andy has tears in his eyes, but he knows what I think of his dad, so Andy turns away from me. I put my arms around him, and hold him. And while he cries into the crook of my neck, I look around the apartment and wonder if it's worth trying to fix anything. We spend two hours in the apartment making paths that go to more debris.

The only restaurant with running water in Santa Monica is La Salsa. It's like a movie set there—fallen buildings in the background and movie stars in the foreground, munching on Mexican food. Andy and I order, but we can't eat. We walk around town looking for the most significant casualty.

At home we try to clean up, but the aftershocks are in the 6.0 range, so everything has to stay on the floor. It gets dark quickly, and since there's no electricity, we go to bed. The building is yellow-tagged, which means it's not condemned—red-tagged—but no one is willing to sign a green tag to vouch that it's safe. We should be staying in a hotel, but that seems like giving up. So we lie on our pillows, and when there's a 3.0 aftershock, we don't move, and when there's a 5.0, we go to the doorway.

I realize that I am lying there in bed, next to Andy, hoping for another 7.4, but I know it won't happen again. Not for me and Andy.

I ORGASM with a penis. Most women need a tongue. Allie needs a tongue.

Allie tells me when Rodrigo first started fucking her, he kept talking about how great it would be for them to come at the same time. She told him his penis is not the center of the universe, and it has nothing to do with her orgasms, and if he wants to come when she does, he should jerk himself off while he's going down on her.

I think about Allie and how powerful Allie must feel when Rodrigo goes down on her. I decide this is going to be the night I tell Andy he has to go down on me because his penis is not the center of the universe. But I come when he comes, and for those seconds his penis *is* the center of the universe. I tell him to go down on me. But when I send his head down to the end of the bed, he feels so far away.

MIKE IS ANDY'S BROTHER, and Karen is the woman he lives with. They call each other honey and sweetie. I want to talk about Karen's last husband, who locked her in a room with him and then shot himself, but Karen and Mike want to talk about their politics, which worries me because it's a ten-hour drive to Andy's mom's house. I notice Mike did all the packing. I notice "honey" is a nice preface to, "You forgot to pack my clipboard." Mike says that after Karen finishes her PhD in physics, she's going to help him run political campaigns.

I ask, "Was your last husband involved in politics?"

Karen says, "It's a long story."

Andy, who is gripping the steering wheel too tightly, says, "I brought some chocolate to keep us awake for driving. Look in the cooler."

Everyone wants chocolate. I pass the box to the back, and Karen says, "Oh, honey, do you want to share the heart?" Then she pokes her head in between the front seats. "Do you guys mind if we eat the heart? It's our year anniversary since the first time we rode in a car together."

I ask Andy if he wants to share, but he says he's sick of chocolate.

I tell everyone I have to go to the bathroom. We stop at a rest place that is not really a rest place, because there are piles of shit on the grass that people have tracked on the sidewalk, so you have to be on guard.

When we get back in the car, I notice Mike has m&m's. I wait to see if he offers us some, but he doesn't. "Mike," I say, "are you eating food that we don't know about?"

"Oh. I didn't know you'd want some."

Andy says it's my turn to drive. He says, "Please don't drive too fast."

"Look," I say, "it was okay for you to show me the mechanical stuff when I was learning to shift, but I think I can handle the speed limit."

"I find if I stay at about sixty, I don't get tickets," he says.

I say, "Thank you for sharing that with me, honey."

It's dark when I start driving and I can barely see the road. I follow a car that's the same make as Andy's and this way I can go faster because I don't have to see the road, just the taillights.

"Karen, what about that story?" I say. Andy glares at me.

"If you don't like to talk about it," I say, "I'll understand, I'm just really curious."

"I've told it so many times," she says, "I don't mind talking about it." She starts to tell me the story, but I've already heard it, so I interrupt. "What made you stay with him?"

"We had a lot of fun together. He was really good to me, just really possessive. I didn't like the possessive part, but I was too scared to leave. I would think about leaving but I never did it. When I told him I was thinking about leaving, just to try to get used to the idea myself, he shot himself."

"How was he good to you?"

"He was very supportive. Like, he left his job in Texas so we could move to Minnesota, where I wanted to go to school."

"That was nice. Was there blood?"

"When he shot himself?"

"Yeah."

"No, just in a small puddle by the door. He stood against the door when he shot himself. So he fell in front of the door. My first reaction was that I'd be stuck in the room. But I was able to drag his body away and get out. That was the bloody part."

By the time the story's done, my eyes are used to driving, and I go very fast, fast enough to pass. And Andy's too tired to say anything.

I READ A SURVEY that says college-educated women receive oral sex twice as often as non-college-educated women. I am in graduate school. I am not receiving all the benefits of my education.

ALLIE AND I are in the basement of my building reading Sylvia Plath and doing Andy's laundry. It's a tiny room with no chairs, so we sit on the floor next to each other against the dryers and it's warm and cozy and Allie's voice is in perfect pitch with the hum of the dryers.

Allie says if I keep doing Andy's laundry I'm going to kill myself like Sylvia Plath.

I tell Allie the wash is just a favor, it has nothing to do with gender.

Allie says I'm deluding myself.

I tell Allie I think my breasts are starting to sag.

"Starting?" she says. "Mine are totally sagged."

"I'm sure they're not totally sagged," I say, "it's scientifically proven that breasts are not totally sagged when you're twenty-six years old."

"No, look," she says, and turns her body to face mine, and I look, and I'm looking at her bra, which is white and lacy, and I'm thinking how would it be to see under her bra when she lifts up her bra, and there her breasts are. They're bigger than I expected—bigger than mine, and her nipples are big, and pinkish brown and everything is smooth and round.

She pulls her bra down and then her shirt. "So?" she says.

"What?" I ask.

"Do you think they sag?"

"I can't remember."

"What do you mean you can't remember?"

"What do you mean flashing me like that?"

"I didn't flash you. It's just my breasts. Girls always show their friends their breasts. I've done it my whole life."

"But not like this," I say. "I looked lustfully, not informatively. You knew that would happen."

Allie says, "You're overreacting,"

That night, we double date. Allie won't go out at night without Rodrigo, so I bring Andy along to talk to him. Then I can talk to Allie, or I can talk to Andy while Allie drools over Rodrigo in the backseat.

We pick them up and go to a cafe. Allie and Rodrigo want to play this game where one person names three actors or actresses and everyone else has to guess what movie they're in. Allie thinks Rodrigo is a genius because he can stump everyone. Andy and I are losing because we don't even know who the people are, let alone what movie they're in. I keep getting up to do stuff—bathroom, extra silverware, etc.—so I don't have to watch. When it's my turn, I say, "Maureen McCormick, Eve Plumb, and Susan Olsen."

Allie tells me *The Brady Bunch* doesn't count, and I'm ruining the game. She apologizes to Rodrigo.

Andy asks Rodrigo why he wants to make films. I put my hand on Andy's hand and I squeeze. Rodrigo says he likes films because of the editing room: "You can make something out of nothing," he says. "You can lie."

I take an olive off Allie's plate, and she glares at me. She offers Rodrigo some olives.

We drop Allie and Rodrigo off at Rodrigo's apartment. I get out of the car to let them out of the backseat. I lift up my shirt. No bra.

ANDY WANTS TO STOP analyzing every fight we have. I would've thought he would have missed the analyzing while I was away at school, but I guess that's not happening. He says, "I want to lighten up the relationship—have some fun once in a while."

"Analyzing is fun," I say.

He frowns.

"Look," I say, "I'm not the fun type. Don't be trying to make me into the fun type."

He says, "I'm not asking for you to be the fun type. I just think we could spend less time talking about the relationship and more time having it."

This idea sounds sinister to me, but I can't argue with it. We go out for ice cream.

We get in the car and there's a whole new selection of CD's that he bought while I was at school. I put in Johnny Cash.

"You like him?" Andy asks.

"I heard him on the U2 album."

The first line of the first song is something like, It could've been great if I hadn't killed her. I skip track one. "Why did you buy this stupid CD?" I say. "You're encouraging Johnny Cash to write songs about killing women."

We get to the ice cream place, and we order, but eating ice cream with Andy is not very appealing.

DAVID CALLS to tell me that I missed the biggest snowfall of the whole year.

"Save some in your freezer for me," I say.

"No. That always sounds like a good idea, but the snow is never fun when you go back to it."

"Oh."

"How's Andy?"

"Same as the snow."

"Big fall?"

"No. Not as good when you go back to it."

"Like what?"

"I don't want to talk about it. What have you been doing?"

David summarizes his sexual escapades making them seem non-sexual. At this point, I know him well enough; walking someone home at midnight means shtupping him.

I ask David if he's a bottom or a top. He says he doesn't want to tell me, and I tell him that's stupid, because I tell him everything.

"But I don't ask," he says.

I say, "You can learn a lot about someone from their sex life."

"No."

"Then I'm just assuming you're a bottom. Remember the book you gave me, *Spontaneous Combustion*? The guy in that book goes on a phone sex line, and everyone's looking for tops, and he says there's always a shortage of tops."

"That's just fiction. I'd never have given you the book if I'd known you'd use it as the Bible for gay life."

"Well?"

"Okay. I'm neither. I mean, I'll do either one, it depends on the circumstances."

"Oh. Well, let's say there's a guy on the bottom, with a penis in him. Will he be able to come without touching his own penis?"

"Each case is different."

"You can't keep answering like that. It's not helpful. These are nonanswers."

"I don't just go around talking about this stuff. You talk about it all the time."

"Oh, so you're hoarding your sexual knowledge? You're giving it false value. At least I'm not so egotistical that I think every sexual thing I do is this huge juicy secret."

"It feels weird telling you stuff because I'm used to telling guys."

"I can relate. I know what it's like to have a penis up my ass."

"Oh god. I don't want to hear about it."

RODRIGO BROUGHT a picnic lunch to Allie's work and they shared it. Rodrigo brought a tube of cookie dough to Allie's apartment and they baked it.

Allie tells me about the night she and Rodrigo took a bath together. I can't stand it anymore. I go home and tell Andy: "Last night Rodrigo brought Allie a pint of ice cream and they took a bath with pink bubbles and peach oils and Allie ate Cherry Garcia off Rodrigo's penis."

"I asked you to do that once," Andy says. "Remember?"

"Oh, yeah."

"You didn't want to."

"Oh, yeah. But the ice cream didn't have Nutrasweet. Regular sugar isn't sweet enough for me anymore."

"What if we bought some fake ice cream and tried again?"

"No. Forget it."

ANDY IS LEAVING. I can tell. We have plans to meet eight people at a restaurant for Andy's birthday. It's a surprise, but I told him, because I'm not in the mood for surprises.

These people are all my friends, but they work for Andy, so they won't be my friends after Andy dumps me. Jon and Elisabeth were my friends before I even knew Andy. This is the biggest rip-off of all.

At the table, I'm silent, and Andy's making jokes. Andy never makes jokes. All the other people at the table are playing with their silverware. Jon says to me, "So, are you excited to go back to Boston?"

"Yes," I say.

Jon says, "I thought you didn't like it there."

I go to the bathroom. I pick the handicapped stall because I need the space. I sit on the toilet and cry. Elisabeth knocks on my door. I let her in, and she says, "You're so sad. Is this about the same thing as last week?"

"No," I say. I don't tell her that this week I'm crying because it's Andy who wants to break up. We would look too unstable. She hugs me. When Andy and I break up, she'll see Andy all the time and I won't.

"Yeah," says Andy. He pushes the comforter off of our bodies even though it's winter. "I can tell you now."

I'm cold with just the sheets, but it's too late to complain. "Okay," I say, and we lie there, and I know he's trying to figure out how to say it. My mind starts racing, thinking of things he's maybe going to say to me, but I don't want to think about what he doesn't like about me because fuck him, I can't always be changing for him. So I think about how awful my brother's wedding is going to be if I have to go alone. I won't be able to offset my pink satin bridesmaid's dress and peach silk bouquet with a clean-shaven head, because being a rebel is cool when you have a serious boyfriend and lonely when you don't, because in that case, you probably won't. People will say: "Marc is so happy, too bad for his sister." And I will have to waltz with uncles and fox-trot with cousins, and no amount of alcohol will make up for having to sit at a table with my parents. And my relatives will say, "I'm sorry to hear about Andy," even though they're not, because he's not Jewish, and I'll say, "Well, at least I didn't stay with him and have an unconscious, conventional relationship like you." And then I'll drink more, and more, and I'll go to the hotel lobby and call Andy and scream at him that he's ruining this wedding and he's ruining my life and why can't we get back together.

Andy wraps his leg around mine, and asks, "What are you thinking about?"

I wrap my fingers around his and say, "I have to get out."

▼

WE KNOW it's going to be our last fuck. I'm feeling sentimental about it and I tell him we have to refer to it as making love. I'm feeling sentimental about love, and I tell myself my next lover and I will always refer to it as making love.

I let my clothes drop to the floor by the side of the bed.

I tell myself I'm past fucking. But still, we're doing it.

Andy drops his clothes to the floor on his side of the bed. Last night's clothes, and the clothes of almost-last night's cover the floor at the end of the bed.

We lie naked in bed, anticipating last, passionate strokes and loud parting steps. "Should I put some music on?" he asks.

"Did you bring in the Soul Asylum CD?"

"We've been listening to that all weekend," he says.

"I know," I say, "so that CD is ruined for the rest of our lives. Let's not ruin another."

ON THE MORNING that I fly back to Boston, my arms are full of baggage. Andy is carrying baggage too—helping me get it out of the apartment, so he can live without it—at least until spring break. Tears are leaving residue under my contacts, and now everything is cloudy. We're standing at the front door, trying not to drop anything, and he says, "Do you want any pictures?"

I say, "Yes," and I take the one where he's just cut off a cactus fruit with his Swiss Army Knife and holds it up for the camera, and he looks like a total geek.

Today is the same as all other days we said good-bye in airports, except today we're crying harder. On all other days we'd go to a corner to cry while we said good-bye, but today our sadness is too big to hide.

The only way I can leave is to tell myself I'll be back, and that he wouldn't cry this hard if he really wanted to break up.

I settle into my window seat with a blanket in my lap and a pillow to block the view.
I wait for the plane to take off.
After initial turbulence, I put down my tray to write a list—

People who I wish had died instead of me and Andy breaking up:

Everyone.

I'M WATCHING an Alfred Hitchcock film. I watch one Alfred Hitchcock film every week for my Alfred Hitchcock class. We analyze the films in terms of feminism and psychoanalysis. Each week I take the laser disc and a stack of magazines into an audio/visual cubbyhole.
Tonight it's *Notorious*, the third week in a row of Ingrid Bergman getting kissed. I'm sick of seeing Ingrid Bergman kiss.
I read *Wired* magazine so I can keep up with the cyber hipsters.
If the movie moved faster, it might be good. There are lots of psychoanalysis jokes. I look up between paragraphs.
I read *Mix* magazine because I might need to know how to be an audio engineer, and because Andy reads *Mix*. I'm sad that we knew each other so well, and now I'll have to read a whole new set of magazines to understand a whole new person.
Ingrid and Cary kiss, in a basement, and Ingrid is excited, and she moans and runs her hands through his hair.
I read the ads in *Wired*.
I fast-forward to the part where Ingrid and Cary live happily ever

after. Missing everything in between makes their escape together seem stupid. Not totally stupid, but stupid enough so that I think it could happen to me, too.

DAVID AND I go to the club in Provincetown where David used to tend bar. He says that during the winter it's empty, except for this weekend, which is President's weekend, when people come to find summer rentals. "You have to do it early," David says.

We sit in the apartment until midnight, waiting for the bar to fill up. It's an hour past my bedtime. I say I'll go for twenty minutes, just to see what it's like.

Every guy David walks by says hi to him with a smile.

I sit by the dance floor and David gets himself bottled water. His huge muscles and boring, tidy lumberjack clothes look awkward in the straight world, but here they look good. Here David has the confidence of Scarlett O'Hara, and the room is full of gay Ashley's, staring David down.

When David goes to get another bottle of Perrier, I am a speck on the wall. But when David comes back, I am standing with the most popular guy, so I stay a little longer.

David can't stand still. I bounce around next to him. He says he wishes he were tending bar because it seems so dumb to just stand around when he could be getting paid to be there.

The guy standing behind David grabs his butt. I don't think David's butt is that great—it's sort of big, from all his muscles. David spins around and says, "Did you just grab me?"

The guy plays dumb. "I think it was my friend," he says.

David says, "If I were you I wouldn't call someone who would do that my friend."

The guy stands there sort of smiling.

David says, "Do you know not to do that again? Do you? Yes? No? Do you know not to do it again?"

The guy says, Yes.

David walks away, nose in the air.

I follow, two steps behind.

ALLIE CAN'T GET THE NEEDLE in her arm herself, so Rodrigo does it, which makes me sick, but I am trying not to be judgmental. "How does this help get the egg out?" I ask.

"I don't know," Allie says, "the hormone shots make the egg loosen or something and then the doctors pull it out with a tweezers."

"Tweezers?"

"Well, a big tweezers. I don't know. It doesn't hurt. That's what they say."

"But there will be little Allies all over the planet."

"Probably just one little Allie, and I'll never see her."

"Don't the hormones mess you up?"

"Who knows? If they do mess me up, I'll have a great PowerBook for recording the experience."

"Allie, this is prostitution. This is letting men buy you."

"This is beating the system. Most women endure months and months of premenstrual hell, and then they end up giving their eggs to men for free. Rodrigo says it's a turn-on that I know how to get what I want with my body."

ANDY CALLS ME up for a chat. It's a scheduled chat. That's how we do it now that we're broken up.

I pick up the phone on the sixth ring, so I seem busy.

I talk about facts. One of the reasons Andy cited for breaking up is that my emotions are too big for him. I ask what he's been doing since I went back to school, and he says, "I read the book you recommended."

"Which one?" I recommended about 400 books to him because he reads only one book a year, and it's usually crap, like Tom Robbins, or John Dewey—stuff he never finishes. I've been telling him for two years that if he'd start the books I recommend, he wouldn't stop in the middle.

"*Waiting For The Barbarians*," he says, "and also that Marguerite Duras book, and a book by Tom Robbins."

He's expecting me to tell him Tom Robbins sucks, so I say, "That's a lot of reading for four days."

"Not really," he says, "*Waiting For The Barbarians* is short."

Fuck you, I think, Why don't you admit that reading is the only way to keep your mind off me? "What did you think of it?" I say.

"I liked it."

"Yeah? How did you like the part about the guy who gets all his emotions from the woman and the whole time he's hating her for being too dependent on him?"

"What?"

I feel my anger coming. I know it's too big. I click the hang up button once, quickly. "That's call waiting," I say, "I have to go. I have to see who's calling."

I WATCH AT THE TRAIN STOP. I watch at the coffee shop. I'm even watching when I'm running. I'm watching time pass, and in class, today, I am so busy watching time pass that I don't notice we are seeing a laser disc of *Rear Window*, until the teacher says,

"Let's skip to the kiss," and he zaps the laser disc to Grace Kelly's red lips.

A student says, "This is the most perfect kiss in Hollywood," and I feel sick, and I want the whole world to stop kissing until enough time passes. Excuse me, I want to say, and the teacher would pause the disc. Excuse me, but this is not a perfect kiss. This is a social construct of a kiss. Her lipstick doesn't even get on his face. I don't raise my hand, though, because I don't want to pause. I don't want the wait to be any longer than it needs to be.

"Notice," he says, "when Grace returns to her man after being across the courtyard. His eyes light up. This is when he decides he loves her."

I think of my return to L.A. at spring break. I skip ahead to March:

I get off the plane and Andy is waiting there and we kiss and he tells me he wants to get back together.

Pause.

Skip back.

I get off the plane, and my hair is cut perfectly—cut twice, for fifty bucks a pop because I know I have to look perfect to make Andy's eyes light up. We kiss, and he tells me he wants to get back together.

Pause.

Skip back.

I get off the plane, and my hair is cut perfectly—cut twice, for fifty bucks a pop because I know I have to look perfect to make Andy's eyes light up. We kiss, but it's a halfhearted kiss because I don't want to appear too eager, and Andy had no idea I would kiss him. He tells me he wants to get back together.

Pause.

Skip back.

I get off the plane, and my hair is cut perfectly—cut twice, for fifty bucks a pop because I know I have to look perfect to make Andy's eyes light up. We kiss, but it's a halfhearted kiss because I don't want to appear too eager, and Andy had no idea I would kiss him. He tells me he wants to get back together, and he knows it would be torture for us both to stay in the apartment for the week, so he's leaving L.A. for my spring break.

The teacher says, "We should remember that in the end, Grace manipulates him to think he's getting what he wants, but he'll never be happy." The teacher says we're running out of time, but for me, it's going backwards, and there's no end in sight.

I FLY TO ILLINOIS for Marc's wedding, which I feel like we have been preparing for since the beginning of time. His fiancée is Orthodox, and so is the wedding. The ceremony is in Hebrew, and no one in our family knows what's being said.

The dances are Israeli, and my family has never heard this music in our lives. We spread out in secret places like the bathroom or the lobby or our cars.

Marc dances. Then he gives a speech about how wonderful the Orthodox life is because the focus of Judaism is on family togetherness.

I DON'T CARE if I'm in Boston right now. I want the Santa Monica apartment. I want a job. I want money. I don't want to cry again when I think about giving back Andy's Gold Card.

This is what I tell myself when I'm preparing for Andy's end-of-the-week phone call.

I tell him I think we shouldn't talk for a month. I need a chunk of time to separate my life from his.

He cries. He says he knows that's a good idea, but it makes him sad.

We talk about how we're doing. He's going to parties, and when people ask how the long-distance relationship is going, he says, It's okay.

So I feel safe saying I have to call a friend every night for a pep talk. "I'm hoping I won't be sad forever," I say.

He says, "I'm trying hard not to make a schedule for my feelings. I'm just letting my feelings happen."

"Oh."

Silence.

I say, "Let me tell you the days I'm coming home for spring break." I am careful to call Santa Monica my home so he doesn't feel too possessive of the apartment.

"I'm still sort of fuming about the apartment," he says. "I think you're being unreasonable."

The apartment is rent control, and you pretty much have to be the producer of *Star Wars* to have enough connections to score a rent control apartment in Santa Monica. I can think of a million arguments about why I should get the apartment, like we wouldn't have it if I hadn't given the landlord's son a hand job the month before I met Andy. So while he is saying how important it is for him to have the apartment so he can walk to work, I'm thinking about my choices. I can fight hard for the apartment, or I can act like I really want the apartment and then give in, out of compassion for Andy's need to walk to work, and then when I'm applying for jobs, maybe he'll vouch that I produced CD-ROMs for his company. Or at least designed them.

I decide to hedge. He deserves this—he hedged during the whole two years of the relationship. "I see where you're coming from," I say, "and I hope you can understand what I'm saying, too. Why don't we brainstorm over the next few weeks for a solution we can both feel okay with?" I am so impressed with how rational I sound.

"That sounds like a good idea," he says.

Then, out of nowhere, I start getting really teary, and I say, through sobs, "I know it's hard to believe, but I really care about you and I don't want to screw you with the apartment, and I really want a production job."

THE DEADLINE for throwing people out of school for being virally dangerous is coming up, so I walk to the infirmary to get a TB shot, and by the time I get there, I'm crying. "I need a shot," I say. "I am one of those people who cries."

"I see," says the nurse. "Why don't you look away?"

"This is part of it," I say. "I hate the kind of person who would look away instead of cry."

"Oh," she says, and rears back to stab me.

"No, wait," I say from behind my Kleenex. "You have to say 1 . . . 2 . . . 3 . . . then do it. Okay? Don't go 1 . . . 2 . 3stab. There has to be rhythm."

She obliges.

As soon as it's over, I take a deep breath. I notice a speck of blood. "Don't I need a Band-Aid?"

"If you want one, sure. Do you need one with stars?"

"Okay."

"We only have plain." She puts it on, but one corner sticks to itself, and I know it's going to come off soon, but I'm not crying.

THE PHONE RINGS as I'm going out the door, but I answer because it might be Andy.

It's Allie, and it's the first time she's called in two months.

I tell her I'm on my way out, and she should call me back when she's ready to stop blowing me off.

She says she's totally depressed because she's sure Rodrigo is going to cheat on her. He tells her he's not and she takes that as a sign that he's a pathological liar. "He's ruining my life," she says. "No, he's not ruining my life. He is my life. I can't have men in my life because I have no life when I have a man."

To me, this is an apology for not having called for so long. I take off my coat and sit down to listen.

Allie says Rodrigo's roommate is moving out and she wants to move in because then Rodrigo can't do anything without her knowing about it.

I wonder if she'll bequeath to me her rent control apartment.

I say, "He can still cheat on you, he'd just have to go to the other person's house."

"Do you think he's cheating?"

"No. I don't."

"Do you think I should move in?"

"Yes," I say, "even if it turns out you split up. I learned a lot from living with Andy."

"Thanks," she says, "that's what I wanted to hear."

I PUT ON MY TIGHTEST, sexiest black shirt, even though it's dirty—it only smells in the armpits, and he won't get close enough to notice.

I finagle my way past the department secretary to the office of the chairman of the computer science department, and I catch him at his desk: Tom. "Tom," I say.

Tom says, "There she is, and I haven't returned any of her calls."

I say, "Yeah, I tried not to take it personally." I smile like I'm joking, but I'm not. I tell him I like his haircut. I say, "I have the tape, but it needs editing because my boyfriend, Andy, and I broke up, in the middle, and every edit was torture."

I look closely at Tom. He says, "Do you know how much a DAT machine costs?"

I think he's joking. I think he's telling me he can't edit my tape. "No," I say.

"Well, why don't you find out, and I'll give you a check to buy one?"

We talk about what the art is going to look like on-screen, and he suggests I take digital pictures. I say I'd love to take pictures.

"What comes to mind to take pictures of?" he asks.

"Nudes," I say festively.

"Great, if you can get people to pose." A normal person would think this is a bore, but Tom is an engineer, and after dealing with Andy for two years, I know they're repressed.

"Would you like to pose?" I ask. "I'll do them in soft focus so no one can tell."

"I would if it weren't for my position," he says, turning red. Or maybe he was already a little ruddy, but I see him turning red—flattered red. Ripe-to-eat red.

I am so giddy I have shifted in my chair six times in sixty seconds. I see I have to wind things up. "Well, I'm sure I'll find someone to pose," I say. "But remember, I already have those images on the Syquest from L.A." Now I will use *from L.A.* as a euphemism for Andy.

"Then we just need to get that DAT player," Tom says.

"Okay," I say. I'm already standing up because I don't want him to think I'm overstaying my visit. "Thanks," I say.

On the way home, on the train, we kiss. He's nervous, and his face is red, but then he puts his hands on my waist and pulls me toward him, and it feels nice to be touched.

And then I think about talking to Andy while Tom is in my bedroom, waiting, and I don't feel sad talking to Andy, and it seems too fast, like I want to feel a little more sadness before that phone call.

When I get home, I leave a message on Andy's machine asking him what a DAT player costs.

THERE'S A GORGEOUS GUY who is watching us. I assume he's watching David because whenever I'm with David, the men around us are gay and I am irrelevant, but David says the gorgeous guy is watching me. I get excited. I need to be watched.

I tell David to go to the bathroom so I can test the gorgeous guy. The gorgeous guy looks up at me and I look at him and he smiles and I have to look away. I have to look busy, so I start shuffling papers, which all fall on the floor. I look up to see if he saw. He saw. He winks.

David comes back and I rehearse my speech 400 times: Hi. Here's my phone number if you want to call.

I ask David if I wrote my name and number in erotic handwriting. David says I should write David's name and number on the back in case the guy is gay.

David is staring. "Don't stare," I say. "He's not gay."

I do my speech and leave before the gorgeous guy can say anything but thanks.

He doesn't call. The next day he doesn't call again.

I have to see him constantly at my cafe. I should have known better than to hit on someone I practically live with.

He continues to stare at me. He continues to be gorgeous. I hate him.

I make David go to my cafe again so David can see that the gorgeous guy is still staring.

David says he's gay.

I say he's gay, too.

When we walk out, the gorgeous guy watches us. I plant a huge kiss on David's cheek so the gorgeous guy thinks David's my boyfriend and the note was a joke.

"I BROKE UP with Rodrigo."

"Allie, what happened?"

"He's not going to save me, so he's not interesting anymore."

"I know the feeling."

"That's why I love you."

"We'll save ourselves. We'll have a great time when I get back to L.A."

"Do you think so? Do you think we've learned anything? I feel like I keep making the same mistakes, I just see them better after doing them for a while."

"That's why I love you. That's so honest. Everyone else would say—we broke up, but we learned a lot."

I KNOCK ON DAVID'S DOOR at 6 a.m. to say good-bye. He is awake and has just finished making me farewell muffins. They are warm. He lets me hug him because no one is looking.

I have shipped my stuff so I get on the T with just two bags.

Allie meets me open-armed at the Los Angeles airport.
We hold each other.
We have no car to get back to her apartment, in a town that's
built for cars, but at least I can carry my own baggage.

acknowledgements

THANKS TO Susanna Kaysen for a sharp eye and sharp wit and lots of warm dinners. Thanks to Leslie Epstein for plucking me from a pile and giving me a year to breath. Thanks to Jim Krusoe for editorial insight, steady encouragement and a shoulder to lean on.